Julian and Thea walked back to the lifts; two nurses joined them. Thea felt she was living through some strange dream, until reality struck as they reached the hospital doors.

'We'll have to get them to call a taxi,' said Julian, and for the first time a wry expression touched his lips.

'Oh, of course,' said Thea, grateful for the mundane. 'No cars.' They returned to the hospital.

'I'll get two taxis,' Julian said without hesitation. 'One to take you home. I shall go back to The Drive and give Lionel the details. We shan't get a firm diagnosis until she's had more tests. Thank you for your support, Thea—it's been a great help.'

Did he, she asked herself rebelliously, realise just how closely he had associated himself with Vicky? Or how obvious he had made the familiarity of the doctor-patient relationship? In addition, came the critical thought, what had it to do with her?

Sonia Deane is a widow with one son, lives in the Cotswolds, and has written over 120 books. The Doctor Nurse stories were fortuitous. She chose a doctor hero and from then her readers wanted a medical background. Having personal friends who are doctors enables Sonia Deane's research to be verified. She has also been out with an ambulance team and donned a white coat in hospital.

Her previous novels include *Doctor's Forbidden Love*, *Doctor Deceived* and *Doctor's Love Affair*.

DOCTOR ACCUSED

BY
SONIA DEANE

MILLS & BOON LIMITED
ETON HOUSE 18–24 PARADISE ROAD
RICHMOND SURREY TW9 1SR

*First published in Great Britain 1988
by Mills & Boon Limited*

© Sonia Deane 1988

*Australian copyright 1988
Philippine copyright 1988
This edition 1988*

ISBN 0 263 76129 0

Set in 10 on 12 pt Linotron Times
03–0788–51,275

*Photoset by Rowland Phototypesetting Limited
Bury St Edmunds, Suffolk*

Made and printed in Great Britain

CHAPTER ONE

DR JULIAN FRASER said sternly, 'You'd no right to deliver the Manfield baby, Nurse Craig. You're our practice nurse, not a qualified doctor!'

Thea Craig flashed back, 'But I *am* a qualified midwife.' She had expected praise and approval; disappointment sharpened her words. 'You were at your hospital clinic and your cousin was on a midder.'

'You could have got hold of Basil Shaw—you know we have a reciprocal arrangement with him.'

'I tried, but he'd been called to a coronary.' She added swiftly, 'The baby was three weeks early and Mrs Manfield was alone.'

He insisted unreasonably, 'These home births are always a hazard.'

Thea persisted, 'That's not the point. The important thing is that mother and son are both fine, despite being deprived of a *doctor*.' Her scorn denigrated the word.

There was an electric silence while they stood facing each other in his consulting room in Adelaide Crescent, Hove, temperamentally at war. Julian Fraser, thirty-three, with finely etched features, compelling grey eyes, was dominant, often remote; a man everyone wanted to get to know without succeeding, since it was impossible to gauge his thoughts, intentions, or desires. His enigmatical smile was rare, but compelling and an assessment. Now he was challenging, his eyes meeting Thea's with critical surveillance.

'Nevertheless, Nurse Craig (it was only in rare unexpected moments that he used her Christian name), you have recently been inclined to exceed your authority. When my cousin and I require extra help, we'll make the necessary arrangements.'

Thea thought swiftly that his cousin, Dr Robert Fraser, would have supported her. She smarted under the summing up, persisting doggedly, 'When I came here six months ago, you impressed on me that I was free to take the initiative and attend to any cases within my capacity. My aim has been to spare you and Dr Robert. This was an emergency.'

His deep voice softened slightly.

'I don't overlook that.'

Robert Fraser came in at that moment. He was the antithesis of Julian and had the air of an actor, his good looks along film-star lines, and he knew how to pander to the patients, who stood a little in awe of Julian, while recognising that he was a master in his field of gynaecology and a respected consultant at the Mid-Sussex Hospital. Their practice was highly successful and their rooms impressive, with large windows overlooking the sea which, at that moment, was like a deep blue skating rink, studded with stars as the April sun danced on it.

Robert's gaze went straight to Thea. He was aware, as always, of her beauty. She had a *joie de vivre*; a rich golden tan darkened her lustrous blue eyes and emphasised the fairness of her hair. She did not look twenty-four and the curves of her supple body were sensuous and alluring. He said, conscious of the tense atmosphere, 'I've just heard from Enid (their receptionist) that you delivered the Manfield baby and that everything is fine. Congratulations. Pity we can't have some champagne to celebrate.' The words fell incongruously.

Julian ignored that as he addressed Thea. 'Who's at the Manfield house now?' Their gaze met and for a second emotion stirred.

'Nurse Stevens.' Thea added swiftly, 'I got in touch with her the moment I knew that Mrs Manfield's scheduled nurse couldn't leave her present case until early next week. Fortunately Nurse Stevens had just finished with a patient and was free.'

Robert commented with marked approval, 'You certainly took care of everything.' As he spoke he shot Julian a disapproving glare, sensing his mood.

Julian moved from the window where he had been standing, returned to his desk and dialled Mrs Manfield's number, then, 'This is Dr Fraser . . . Ah, Nurse Stevens . . . thank you for helping out. I'll be along shortly.' The house was in Palmeria Square, a matter of minutes away.

Nurse Stevens, a highly efficient SRN, said stoutly, 'It's Nurse Craig you should thank, Dr Fraser. She was splendid.'

'I'm sure she was,' said Julian and, after a few more questions and answers, he replaced the receiver.

Robert exclaimed significantly, 'I hope you appreciate Thea's initiative. A fine recommendation if a patient of yours had been alone when her offspring was born!' In fairness, however, he knew that Julian was always meticulous when it came to his patients, particularly those he had agreed to deliver.

There was a heavy silence which Julian broke, conscious of Thea's unnerving gaze.

'I appreciate everything Nurse Craig does in the interest of the practice.'

'Good of you.' Robert made the comment sound withering. Actually, Julian and Robert worked in harmony: they were good friends as well as relatives, becoming partners when Julian took over the Adelaide Crescent practice from Dr Donaldson with whom Julian had worked for five years. Their respective parents and relatives lived in Somerset, Fraser and Fraser being family solicitors in Taunton. Julian and Robert were both only children and had gone to boarding school together. A question of opposites complementing each other. Julian's absorption with medicine had proved infectious, and Robert had followed him in the profession.

Julian ignored the remark and said politely to Thea, glancing down at a pile of letters on his desk, 'I've signed these; would you take them to Miss Jenkins?'

Thea nodded her assent, but their gaze lingered and she felt a tremor as the power of his somewhat forbidding attraction quickened her heartbeat. Their fingers touched as she took the mail, forcing herself to escape from her conflicting thoughts by concentrating on the fact that Miss Jenkins, their secretary, would hate being deprived of collecting it, which she did as a ritual so that she would have a few precious seconds with Julian with whom she had been in love from the moment she met him when he joined her former employer, Dr Donaldson. She fondly believed that no one suspected this devotion and made a valiant attempt at concealment. She was in her early forties and endured secret humiliation because she was wise enough to realise that the situation was incongruous. She had an old-fashioned air of dignity and neatness which made her appear older than her years, and was an expert secretary, invaluable in the practice. It was always, 'Ask Miss Jenkins'; 'Miss Jenkins will know'. She was far too thin, with wispy fine hair, sallow skin and pale grey eyes, but liked and appreciated by everyone.

Thea went down in the lift to the office and surgery quarters, aware of the shadow that passed over Miss Jenkins' face as she took the post, while managing a gracious smile. Enid Walters looked on, conscious of the little drama. She was an attractive twenty-two-year-old, with naturally curly auburn hair and dark brown eyes, vivacious, modern. She never teased Miss Jenkins about Dr Fraser, respecting her secret.

The door bell went and Enid groaned.

'If that's an emergency, I shall scream! I've just seen the last patient out for today.' She sighed, but hurried to answer it.

'Mrs *Holford*!' she exclaimed, surprised; appraising the elegantly dressed girl of twenty-three whose clothes always had the style and simplicity associated with *haute couture*. 'You're back.' She hastened, 'A silly remark, since you're here!' It struck her that Vicky Holford didn't look as though she had recently returned from a two months' convalescence cruise after a miscarriage.

'Is Dr Julian in? I know it's past surgery time, but I thought I might catch him.'

'You have,' Enid assured her, knowing that the Holfords were his and Robert's friends, and of Thea's too. Lionel Holford, Vicky's husband, was the last man, Enid always thought, to have attracted someone of Vicky's type. He was austere, hard, but undoubtedly in love with her. Rich; but that was of no consequence since Vicky had been left a considerable fortune when her father died. He had made money in his later years, but Vicky had known near-poverty in her early child-hood which had been spent in a small terraced house amid the back streets of Kemp Town, away from the sea. She had retained a natural frankness and had no preten-tiousness, keeping in touch with her friends of those days, often in defiance of Lionel's wishes, her frank admission about the past often irritating him, since it conflicted with his own affluent one.

Hearing Vicky's voice, Thea joined her in the hall from which the offices, common room and surgery waiting room, radiated. It was a lofty, spacious area, in which the lift was conveniently sited.

'Vicky!' Thea, like Enid, observed the look of strain and general malaise. Thea and Vicky's friendship had originated by professional contact, since Vicky was Julian's patient. He had attended her at the time of her miscarriage some three months previously, and had suggested that a cruise would be beneficial. Lionel, as chairman of a financial firm in the City, was able so to arrange his business affairs that the holiday was possible.

Julian came down in the lift at that moment, grave-faced until he saw Vicky and uttered her name in surprise.

'I thought you weren't due back until Saturday.' His smile concealed a professional concern, as they shook hands.

Vicky gave a little chuckle and looked at him intently.

'I'm flattered that you thought at all . . . no, we arrived last evening. I've been to the hairdressers and thought I'd call instead of telephoning.' She added brightly, 'I knew Thea would be here, even if you were out.' She flashed Thea a little friendly glance.

Thea was watching Julian, trying to assess his reaction to Vicky, both as a patient and a woman. His association with the Holfords had always seemed slightly out of character, for he would appear to have little in common with Lionel and was certainly not the type of man to encourage intimate contact of any kind with the women he treated professionally. As against that, she argued, why had she herself been drawn to Vicky? Julian had never shown any disapproval of their relationship.

'How *are* you?' Julian's voice was serious. 'You certainly haven't put on any weight as I told you to.'

She didn't dismiss the question, but admitted half-apologetically, 'I've been burning the candle at both ends. Very easy on a cruise—and drinking too much . . . You shall have an opportunity to admonish me professionally. I want to make an appointment for next Monday if possible. I'll see Miss Jenkins . . . and that's enough about my health. I'd like you, Thea and Robert to come to dinner on Wednesday—get in a last fling in case you start making rules!'

Julian looked at her indulgently, but with underlying anxiety. He had found it difficult to assess the depth of her disappointment over the miscarriage, or accurately to judge her, other than as a charming, appealing character whose company he found stimulating. His and Robert's relationship with her and Lionel was a pleasant diversion, the doctor-patient element strengthening the tie. The fact that Thea was often included in the social gatherings did nothing to detract from their appeal. He enjoyed Thea's company and appreciated her medical skills, feeling a little churlish at his recent attitude over the Manfield baby.

He accepted Vicky's invitation without hesitation. 'I know I'm free on Wednesday. We can have the calls transferred . . . I can't speak for Robert——'

Thea also accepted, feeling a trifle defiant, adding, 'I'll make your Monday appointment before Miss Jenkins goes . . .'

'If it could be the morning,' Vicky suggested.

'After surgery,' Julian put in as Thea went towards Miss Jenkins' office.

'And I'd like to see *you*, Thea,' Vicky called out, 'if you can spare me a few minutes now.'

'Of course,' Thea replied.

'I'm just going out on a case,' Julian said apologetically, 'or——'

'I didn't really hope to catch you at all,' Vicky added, thinking how attractive he looked in his lightweight grey suit and cream shirt. She gazed at him with a lingering expression of approval. 'See you on Wednesday—about seven? We could have a swim.'

The Holfords had a large house in The Drive, and Vicky preferred the indoor swimming pool to sea bathing, disliking the pebbly beach.

'Splendid!' Julian spoke with enthusiasm as he moved towards the front door.

'And tell Robert not to worry about getting in touch with me. If he can't come I shall understand.'

Thea rejoined them. 'Next Monday at midday,' she said to Vicky.

'Oh, good . . . thank you . . . 'bye, Julian.'

'Take care of yourself.' Julian was not merely mouthing a familiar cliché.

Vicky could have retorted, 'That'll be the day!' but instead, she smiled. 'See you on Wednesday.' She

watched him open the large front door and disappear
into the sunlight, her expression inscrutable.

Thea led the way to her room, which was well
appointed, with barley-white walls, sapphire leather-
upholstered chairs, an examining couch, trolley and
small mahogany desk. A matching self-patterned carpet
gave an air of welcome and removed the bleak formality
of the average area. Thea dealt with most patients at
some time or another, and vetted them to spare both
Julian and Robert from minor ailments, hypochondriacs
and malingerers. She had excellent diagnostic abilities
and ought to have become a doctor.

Vicky sat down in the patients' chair, dropped her
shoulders and sighed.

'Suppose you tell me what's troubling you?' Thea
spoke with gentle encouragement.

'Hypocrisy,' Vicky said promptly.

Thea felt a breath of fear without knowing why. When
it came to it, although she had known Vicky for over a
year and there was a close bond between them, that
still left a great deal to discover. And her absence
during the past months seemed to have threatened their
understanding.

'Hypocrisy?' Thea echoed the word disbelievingly.

'You were so very kind when I lost the baby,' Vicky
went on with seeming irrelevance, 'but I didn't deserve
your sympathy—or anyone else's. I just played a part,'
she hurried on. 'You see, I didn't want a child—at least,
not Lionel's. I don't love him.' A faraway look came into
her eyes. 'There's someone else,' she hurried on, 'but
that's another story.'

Thea was shattered, and while the confession did not
affect her, nevertheless she felt involved by the truth.

She murmured unevenly, 'I'm so sorry . . . I didn't dream——'

'Which goes to show what a good actress I've become! I don't know why I'm burdening you with all this, but I've reached breaking point. The cruise has been ironical—a farce, and I haven't been well——' Vicky hurried on before Thea could question her, 'But I don't want to go into that until Monday when I see Julian professionally. I'm determined to enjoy this week.'

The words, *'There's someone else, but that's another story'*, echoed in Thea's mind with a rather disturbing element; she did not underestimate the trauma associated with an unhappy marriage, and while she had not seen Lionel and Vicky as a romantic couple, she had regarded them as well adjusted, with Lionel a proud and protective husband.

'Have I shocked you?' Vicky cut into Thea's thoughts almost challengingly.

'Doctors and nurses are shock-proof . . . I'm just sorry you've been through such a bad time.' Thea paused.

'I don't like pretending, putting on an act. Lionel buys me everything, but gives me nothing.' Vicky added, 'We live in different worlds . . . yours is an interesting world —worth while,' she said, an envious look in her eyes. 'Working for Julian and Robert . . . Thea,' her voice dropped almost to a note of pleading, 'you'll always be my friend—won't you?'

Again Thea felt a shiver of apprehension; there was something solemn and significant in the words, introducing a deeper element which Thea wanted to avoid. It was pleasant to know Vicky as the friendly patient whom she visited on occasions, sometimes with Julian and Robert, as would be the case this coming Wednesday. But it was another matter to regard the friendship as a commitment.

'Is there any reason why I shouldn't be?' Thea asked evasively, but her gaze was direct.

Vicky answered, her cheeks flushing slightly, 'No; no, of course not, but——'

The telephone went. Thea answered it and said, 'Oh, yes, Mrs Webster; what can I do for you? Blood pressure checked?' She was flicking over the pages of her appointment book as she talked. 'Tomorrow at ten . . . yes, you're quite right. I want to keep an eye on it.' A little chuckle escaped her, as Mrs Webster made a joke. She replaced the receiver and realised with a sense of relief that the call had cut through the previous tension and that Vicky was already getting to her feet.

'I mustn't keep you,' she murmured. 'You must be glad to get away at the end of the day. You have a lot of responsibility, don't you? I've never quite realised all you do in the practice. Do you give injections?'

'Yes; syringe ears, bandage wounds—you name it, I do it.'

'I wish I were clever.' It wasn't a remark soliciting praise.

'We all have talents of some kind,' Thea commented. 'Just a question of what we choose to do.'

Vicky suppressed the instinctive reply, 'I chose to marry a man I didn't love. I've cheated him and myself.' She moved to the door as she said, pausing, 'You're the best friend I have. Being able to talk to you honestly——'

There was something forlorn about her as she stood

there that touched Thea's heart, awakening a sudden unexpected sympathy.

'I'm always here.' She got up from her desk and joined Vicky at the door, studying her very intently as those words, '*There's someone else*', re-echoed disturbingly. 'But, Vicky——'

'Yes?' It was a breathless sound.

'The grass isn't always greener over there.'

A tense silence fell before Vicky exclaimed, shaking her head, 'Love refuses to face up to obstacles.' She added swiftly, 'You must see so much emotional turmoil in your job.'

Thea said fervently, 'Oh, we do; we *do*, I assure you.'

Vicky paled and winced.

'What is it?' Thea asked anxiously.

'Oh, nothing . . . a pain I get . . . Julian will sort me out on Monday!' Vicky made an effort and smiled. 'Until Wednesday.' She kissed Thea's cheek. 'Thank you,' she whispered, and was gone.

Thea returned to her desk and stared out across the sea where red-sailed boats and a variety of other craft painted pictures which might well have been in gilt frames, so familiar was the scene. The expanse of Channel seemed illimitable and the horizon was knife-edged. The rooms were quiet and the hush of the April evening held the magic of spring, with the trees in the gardens a bright young green to frame the sweep of the crescent and give it a grandeur.

Robert's voice at the door made her jump.

'Good heavens, you still here?'

'Too lazy to go home.' Home being a flat in Old Steine which overlooked the fountain and flower-beds near the Palace Pier and Royal Pavilion. 'Actually, I've been talking to Vicky . . . you're invited for dinner on Wednesday—Julian and I are going.'

Robert didn't hesitate. 'Splendid; I'll join you.' He looked puzzled. 'You know,' he went on reflectively, 'I can never quite understand how we've become involved with the Holfords. Oh, that sounds all wrong, but we're not his type and we certainly haven't his money . . . I suppose when it comes to it, Vicky is the one who really counts. She's an attractive, natural person, but very tense.'

Thea raised her eyebrows. Robert didn't miss much.

Julian appeared at that moment, looking from face to face almost suspiciously.

Thea, suddenly nervous, said without preliminaries, 'Robert's free on Wednesday.' There was a note of familiarity in the utterance and she told herself that she had no intention of being patronised by Julian and was more than ready to stand up to him. She recalled her father, Trevor's, words when he first met Julian, 'A man I would trust, but doubt if I'd ever understand.' The opinion struck home and she thought lovingly of Trevor in that moment, for they were very close and she was grateful that he lived in Brighton, within a short distance of her at a flat in Royal Crescent. His friendship, as distinct from relationship, was invaluable. Her mother, Avril, had died two years previously of a pulmonary embolism following an appendix operation. The marriage had not been a happy one and Avril, a rigid disciplinarian, had nothing in common with Trevor's artistic, volatile temperament, or with his profession as an architect. The sadness of her death lay in the fact that she was only fifty and no one, including Thea, experienced any real grief. Her passing had released Trevor from a prison of dullness and mediocrity. Now he was free, his domestic needs were met by an excellent housekeeper, Mrs Kingsley, and he was enjoying life for the first time in many years. He gave Thea love and support without making any demands on her time, or interfering in her affairs, but she knew that should she ever wish to share his home, she had only to move in. Since he was only fifty-two, she hoped he might marry again, for he was an attractive friendly man whom women liked.

Julian looked faintly distracted.

'You mean for Vicky's invitation?' He changed his attitude, aware that Thea was speaking *for* Robert and that there was an element of defiance in her manner. It had never occurred to him before to question the nature of their relationship.

'I'm more intrigued by than involved with the Holfords,' Robert commented honestly. 'Then, I'm off to Bramber to see old Mr Brown. He's staying with his daughter and I think he wants an excuse to get back to Hove.'

'To his hotel?' Julian sounded surprised.

'He likes the Fairview. Every convenience, own suite —no problems. He has his friends around him; goes to concerts and the theatre. His daughter's not only retired from being headmistress of St Jude's, she's retired from life and the old boy finds it deadly dull.' Robert laughed. 'She restricts his drinks—not good for him. He sneaks in a bottle of Scotch! Then she smells it, and there's the devil to pay! He's eighty and he intends to live every minute left to him. She puts him in a glass case and suffocates him. Has him there as a "duty" and he goes for the same reason; but he's always cute enough to feign some minor complaint which I aid and abet. His big moment is when he gets in his car and drives home! Looks like a naughty schoolboy. I can do with Mr Brown!' He glanced at Julian as he reached the door. 'How was Mrs Manfield?' he asked deliberately.

'Fine.'

'Make sure you thank Thea.' He smiled broadly at Thea and added unexpectedly, 'Will you be at home later on?' When she said yes, he asked, 'May I look in for a coffee and drink? I've a case I'd like to discuss with you.'

'Of course,' she agreed, smiling.

'See you later, then.'

When the door closed behind him, Julian said, 'He was quite right about my thanking you. Your patient is splendid . . . I was insufferable about it. God knows why.'

If the vase of flowers on her desk had suddenly started to do the cha-cha, Thea could not have been more surprised by Julian's attitude.

'It wasn't an isolated case, Dr Fraser,' she replied boldly. She studied him as she spoke, aware that there was a certain strain about him, a nervous tension beneath what she felt to be the effort he was making towards conciliation. Her voice held no compromise and her eyes met his levelly and challengingly. Her heart quickened its beat. She was prepared for anything and quite ready to give in her notice. 'I don't like being intimidated,' she added with an impressive calm.

He looked shocked and said involuntarily, 'Thea, I'm so *sorry*.'

A silence fell between them, heavy and disturbing. They looked at each other in faint bewilderment, emotion surging to replace discord.

Thea caught at her breath as she said, 'Suppose we put it down to pressure of work?'

'A very generous summing up . . . You're really indispensable here——' Julian made a gesture to wave aside any protestations. 'I'm serious. We leave so much to you, not only medically but psychologically; you can often deal with the domestic issues far better than either of us, and I'm sure you saved young Alan Baker from suicide after he'd attacked his drunken father. You saw him through the whole case. *We* got the credit. I *think* of you more as a doctor, I assure you.'

Thea laughed. 'Human nature being what it is, probably that was why you didn't like my taking on the mantle *of* one without permission!'

He nodded and gave her an illuminating smile.

'You're a very discerning person—a very remarkable one.' He didn't make it sound like a compliment and there was a genuine assessment in the tone of his voice.

'One would need to be, to work here,' she said, 'or, for that matter, in any medical capacity.' Julian had remained standing, but he suddenly sat down opposite her in the patients' chair. He looked like a man wrestling with some unsolved problem, and uncertain whether or not to discuss it. Then he said, she felt unintentionally, 'You and Robert are good friends.'

The words hung between them and Thea was not quite sure how to react to the obvious statement in which there seemed to be an implicit question.

'One knows where one is with Robert,' she commented somewhat startlingly, the implication obvious.

'But not with me,' he added darkly.

She thought of Trevor's words and sought refuge in evasion.

'Don't put words into my mouth. Robert doesn't take life so seriously.'

'Consequently he hasn't any problems.'

'His temperament doesn't create them.'

'Touché!' The hint of laughter went from his voice as he added jerkily, 'I'm worried about Vicky.'

The words fell almost dramatically on the silence.

'Vicky?' Thea echoed a little fearfully.

'She certainly doesn't look well; she's lost more weight.'

Thea stiffened, not wanting Vicky brought into the conversation.

'Well, she told you she'd been burning the candle at both ends . . . life on a cruise is only as beneficial as you allow it to be. Anyway, you'll be able to set your mind at rest on Monday.' She studied him intently, struck by the intensity of his concern as manifested in his expression and tone of voice. Her own conversation with Vicky did nothing to reassure her. She knew that his assessment was correct.

Julian sighed. 'It's not always a good thing to have one's friends as patients,' he murmured reflectively.

Thea couldn't stay the words, 'That was hardly the case with you.'

His eyes darkened, his exclamation was accusing. 'Meaning?'

'That she was your patient first; the friendship followed.'

He corrected, '*They* were my patients, if you must be so precise.'

They were sliding back to dangerous ground.

'Then shall we say that there are disadvantages in most relationships. It's a question of involvement.' The words came significantly.

Julian's words were clipped. 'She's been through a bad time——'

'*There's someone else; but that's another story*'. Did Julian realise this? Had Vicky confided in him? Thea argued that it was unlikely, or he would not be discussing her case at that level. Her own hands were tied. There was little for her to say. She was grateful that Julian went on, 'I'd hoped the cruise and change of scene would enable her to get over the trauma of the miscarriage——' His expression was questioning; he obviously, Thea knew, wanted her comment and opinion.

She said evasively, 'Another pregnancy might be the answer,' and even as she spoke she heard the echo of Vicky's words, '*I don't want a child—at least, not Lionel's*'. A strange presentiment touched her. Why had Vicky suddenly loomed so large on the horizon, almost as though taking precedence over all other considerations? She watched Julian carefully, her gaze trained on his without gleaning anything of his feelings from his expression, which was suddenly blank. The silence was disconcerting and he got up abruptly from his chair, saying, 'I'm keeping you . . . enjoy your evening.' With that he went from the room.

Thea sat there for a moment staring into space, unable to explain why she should feel so bleak and apprehensive. It struck her that their conversation had petered out to a point where there would have been silence. What was he going to do now? He had a service flat in Ellsmere Court on the front and, since it had a restaurant, was spared all domestic problems. It would be too dramatic to call him a mystery, since his life would appear to be free of all commitments; yet that element of remoteness prevailed, manifesting itself in a certain lack of communication. While he had expressed concern for Vicky, it was impossible to gauge the depth of his anxiety, or his involvement as a friend. She got up from her chair impatiently, realising she was giving him undue importance. He had apologised and that was the end of that. Suddenly, and to her surprise, he reappeared at the door.

'Will you have dinner at the Grand with me next week?'

She raised her eyebrows and gave him a startled look. Apart from the sporadic meetings at the Holfords', there had never been any social contact between them.

'Thank you,' she answered. 'I'd like to.'

'We'll finalise things tomorrow . . . it's time you got away from here, or had you forgotten Robert?' He spoke deliberately.

She had; but didn't admit it as she took her handbag and preceded him out of the door he held open for her.

Outside the tree-lined crescent gleamed cream and white in the bright sunlight, looking down to the sea across four lanes of traffic, and the lawns which led to the slipway, pebble beach and groynes. The Channel was as blue as the cloudless sky and all the buildings as far as the eye could see looked newly-painted and immaculate, the West and Palace Piers jutting out to enhance a scene which retained the splendour of the past Regency days.

Julian saw Thea to her car which was parked near Brunswick Terrace, and at that moment he seemed like a friendly stranger whom she had just met. He could walk to his flat, and he strode out almost before she had moved away. A strange uneasiness stirred as she drove past the Grand. Why should he invite her out to dinner? Abruptly and, obviously, as an afterthought. She heard his words again, '*You're our practice nurse, not a doctor*'. Perhaps he was genuine in the desire to atone for the pointed reminder. Her thoughts raced on. She was glad Robert was calling in, even though she had momentarily forgotten the fact. Their friendship had deepened recently, but she did not want to take it too seriously, any more than she wanted to consider the possibility of marrying Howard Flemming, a cardiologist and family friend—serious, determined, whose devotion had not wavered during the past three years. Trevor was too wise to stress the eminent suitability of such a match, but she knew that he would be delighted should she become Howard's wife. A warmth stole upon her as she thought of him when she let herself into her flat.

The telephone was ringing and she uttered his name with pleasure, adding, 'I was just thinking of you.' She had visions of him, tall, dark, looking handsome in tweeds, his faintly rugged features suggesting the athlete. 'This evening? Afraid not. Robert's coming in for a drink . . . tomorrow? Yes, fine.'

At the other end of the line, Howard added another few words and put the receiver down with a sigh. He didn't conceal his jealousy of Robert, without disliking him. But for Robert, he argued, Thea would agree to marry him. And Robert had the advantage of daily proximity. Julian didn't come into the picture, and he thanked his lucky stars for that, he decided as he poured himself out a whisky.

A little flame of happiness built up as Thea showered and slipped into a flimsy cream summer dress, patterned with blue. The evening was one of those bonuses which the English climate accords when in a generous mood, even if all too rarely. Her sitting room overlooked the gardens which were a blaze of colour, and dominated by the sparkling fountain, its lower base structure resting on the entwined figures of three dolphins which also formed part of the coat of arms of the Borough of Brighton. The flat itself was quaint, with three wide stairs going up to two bedrooms. It was all cream and pale green, with a few antiques to give the furnishing a richness and mellowness which whispered of the past.

Robert arrived early, gazed at her and said, 'You look terrific . . . would you marry me, by any chance?' His voice had dropped to a low, rather husky appeal before he added solemnly, 'I'm serious. This is the only way of plucking up the courage to ask you.'

Thea blinked and sat down abruptly. Surprises seemed the order of the day. She stared at him, bewildered. 'You need courage; I need to get over the *shock*!'

He moved swiftly to sit beside her on the sofa. The sun fell on her shining fair hair, spinning cobwebs of gold upon it. Her skin was fine and slightly flushed; a faint warm perfume stole from her freshly powdered body.

'I love you, Thea——' There was a humble note in his voice.

'Oh, Robert,' she sighed, 'I never dreamed . . . it just hasn't ever crossed my mind.'

He almost growled, 'It isn't easy to be emotional with Julian around. Oh, I don't mean that in a detrimental way, but there's no relaxing . . .' He held her gaze. Waiting.

She didn't know what she felt for Robert, she thought with a degree of panic. He was attractive and could not be dismissed as a friend. His nearness stirred her and when suddenly, gently, but with increasing passion, he took her in his arms, she responded to his kiss and the pressure of his body without resistance. She had never been in love and she drew back, breathless, and told him so, finishing, 'I don't want to settle down; be married and have children . . .'

'Marriage doesn't need to mean settling down,' he insisted, 'and as for having children——' he looked at her intently, '——we can choose our time. So you see, there *are* no problems. Just that one little word, "yes", is all I ask!'

Thea looked down at her hands and clasped them tightly together as if for inspiration. Her lips were still tingling from his kiss; the experience seemed new, for although she had been proposed to twice before, besides by Howard, on neither occasion was there any question of her accepting. She got to her feet restlessly and crossed to the window, then, 'I'm sorry,' she said quietly. 'I'm not sure enough of myself, or of the meaning of the word "love". I don't want marriage until I'm absolutely sure.' She turned and sat down opposite him, her expression serious. 'I want it to be for life, Robert.'

'So do I,' he agreed earnestly. 'Thea—it could be!'

It would all be so simple, she thought; and then Howard came to mind. Only a short while ago she had been thinking of him with affection, but she knew that Robert had touched a chord, awakening a sensuality new and tempting. How easy it would be to confuse it with love, and imperative not to do so.

'I don't want to encourage you—pretend more than I feel,' she said honestly.

He sighed. 'I know.' There was a note of inevitability

in the words. 'We'll leave it for now, only please don't let it make any difference to us—to our friendship.' A half-smile curved his lips. 'What a misnomer that word is,' he added.

'Not really,' she assured him, 'because you *are* my friend, even though we haven't seen all that much of each other, except in a professional capacity. I'd come to you no matter what the trouble might be.' There was a childlike frankness in the utterance.

'I should hold you to that,' he insisted, 'but I hope it will never be necessary.'

Afterwards, she had cause to remember those words.

There was a moment of awkward silence which he broke by saying, 'Howard Flemming wants to marry you, doesn't he? I've only met him on two occasions at your father's flat, but it stood out a mile that he's in love with you.'

Thea's cheeks flushed slightly.

'I'm right?' It was both question and answer. 'I'm bloody jealous!'

'How about pouring us a drink?' she suggested, indicating the tray which stood in an alcove, offering brandy, whisky and sherry.

'Which is about as good a way as any to put an end to this conversation,' he said wryly. 'Ah, well; I can take a hint.' He walked across the room and put two glasses in position. 'Will you come out with me next week?'

Thea agreed, but didn't mention Julian, without quite knowing why.

Thea crossed Church Street from Grand Avenue into The Drive—tree-lined, wide and elegant—and arrived at the Holfords' impressive house with a feeling of suspense and apprehension which amounted almost to presentiment. Briggs, the general factotum, admitted her (he and his wife, Rose, held the reins with the help of a daily and a cook who was on a part-time basis) with a politeness that amounted to a welcome. He had been accustomed to a far higher standard of living in his youth than ever his mistress had enjoyed, and appreciated the fact that Vicky didn't attempt to put on any airs or graces, or even pretend that she was familiar with the luxury in which she now lived.

Vicky appeared almost immediately, her expression faintly disappointed as she said, 'I hope Julian's going to make it. Robert's here. And your father.' She had a loose kaftan-type gown on, the bright red and green emphasising her pallor and the dark rings under her eyes. She had a glass of champagne in her hand and looked, Thea thought, obviously unwell. Julian arrived before Briggs had shut the front door.

Vicky cried, 'I was so afraid you'd be called out!' Her gaze went to his intently.

Lionel Holford came out of the drawing room, disliking Vicky's habit of greeting people almost before they were admitted, instead of waiting for Briggs to announce them. Lionel was a short, brown-haired, impeccably dressed man, inclined to be fussy and meticulously correct. His views and habits were of the old school. He had inherited the family fortune and added to it in the City, secretly craving a more formal social life-style, but too much in love with his wife to make an issue of it.

'Let's go and have a swim,' Vicky said impetuously as Julian and Lionel shook hands.

Julian, like Thea, thought uneasily that Vicky looked

far from well, and that there was an unnatural excitement about her which he did not, rightly, associate with the champagne.

She stopped and added jerkily, 'I've made an awful *faux pas* this evening.'

'How?' Lionel's question was an interrogation.

'Thea and I are the only women in the party and we've four men. I meant to tell Robert to bring a friend and to invite——' she caught at her breath and tensed before adding, 'Marie Young for Trevor.' There was something in her attitude that did not suggest in any way that Julian and Thea should be classed together. 'Ah well, better more men than women.'

She led the way into a large reception room furnished in cream, pale rose and gold. A grand piano stood in a wide bay overlooking the spacious garden, and an oil painting of Lionel's father had pride of place above the chimneypiece while a miniature of his mother adorned a Hepplewhite table nearby. Flowers were set at just the right angles—a tribute to Rose's skill.

Trevor and Robert were talking earnestly and Thea thought how young Trevor looked—grey-haired, but distinguished with a wide encouraging smile that broadened when he saw her. But Thea felt curiously ill at ease. There was something in the atmosphere that disturbed her, and as she intercepted a look between Julian and Vicky, the words came back, '*There's someone else, but that's another story*'.

After a glass of champagne they decided to have a swim. Costumes were in readiness in the cubicles flanking the pool which was large, domed, and tiled in pale aquamarine. There was an air of well-being and extravagance without vulgarity about the embellishment; tables and chairs in white wicker offered sanctuary for those who cared to watch, or rest after the exercise.

'Race you the length,' said Robert as Thea emerged in a brief cream swimsuit that revealed the lines of her perfect figure.

They dived in and swam, Robert winning. Thea looked back to where Julian and Vicky were standing, Vicky far too slim, Julian a fine figure with gleaming tanned skin. Vicky slid into the water and Julian dived in beside her, Trevor and Lionel following. There was laughter, acrobatics and much splashing. Robert kept by Thea's side, but she challengingly struck out and swam towards Julian, whose back was towards her. When she reached him, there was a sudden stirring under the clear water as his hand released Vicky's . . .

But in that second Vicky grasped the side and dragged herself up to the wide tiled terrace, collapsing as she retched and vomited blood.

'My God!' cried Julian, as without hesitation he jumped up beside her. 'Haematemesis!' He turned authoritatively to Thea. 'Look after her . . . ambulance, hospital,' he added, addressing Lionel who had leapt out of the water as Julian hurried to a telephone on a nearby table.

CHAPTER TWO

VICKY was rushed to Casualty at St Stephen's General Hospital. Julian and Thea went in the ambulance. Vicky, vomiting twice during the short journey, managed to whisper, 'Don't . . . want to be . . . alone.' She could hardly think beyond the pain and nausea, but shrank from the solitude of a private room.

Thea was aware of a sense of unreality mixed in with her fear and anxiety. Even in the circumstances she could not erase the picture of Julian's and Vicky's clasped hands beneath the water, or escape from the shock it had given her. She noticed, even now, how tense, even agonised, Julian seemed and how Vicky's gaze had sought his in helpless appeal and a look that could not disguise her feelings, as the ambulance sped, bell ringing . . .

Casualty was momentarily quiet after a hectic early evening, the serious cases put aside to the right of the wide ward-like corridor with its cream walls and bright lights. Short curtains were the only dividing line between trolleys on which stretchers slid, receiving the patients.

Dr Gregory, the senior house officer—young, dedicated to his job—nodded to Julian, whom he knew, and accepted Thea whose name Vicky was whispering. He took in the details of the case and concentrated on Vicky, realising that she was bleeding acutely from somewhere in the upper gastro-intestinal tract and that his first job was to stabilise her condition by sending

31

blood for full blood count, group, cross-match and urea electrolytes. Pending results he put up a drip of normal saline. The volume of vomited blood and an estimation of previous blood loss had to be measured.

Sister Grey, slim, fair and loved by everyone, and Staff Nurse O'Dell, with a rosy-cheeked almost countrified air, assisted automatically, both subconsciously thinking that since Dr Fraser and Nurse Craig were formally dressed, they and the patient must have come from a party. Thea had deftly removed Vicky's swimsuit, put her in the plainest nightdress she could find, and wrapped her in a soft towelling robe, while awaiting the ambulance.

'Get Dr Vaughan.' Dr Gregory looked at Staff Nurse O'Dell who went swiftly away to fetch the Senior Registrar, knowing that it was a question of whether surgery was likely to be required.

Julian and Thea moved outside the curtains and away from the cubicle area, watching Dr Vaughan arrive—a rather solemn-faced man, highly thought of as a surgeon on Mr West's firm.

Behind the curtains, Dr Gregory outlined the case to him, explaining what had been done, adding, 'Pulse a little rapid at 110; blood pressure 100/80.'

Vicky opened her eyes, feeling she was floating in a frighteningly strange world. 'Julian . . . Thea . . .'

Sister soothed her. The two men went outside, joining Julian and Thea.

'Hello, Julian,' Tom Vaughan exclaimed. 'Your patient, I understand?' He courteously repeated Thea's name as Julian uttered it.

Julian's expression asked the question.

Tom Vaughan's voice was steady. 'I think we'll wait

for the blood result before we make a decision about surgery . . . one moment——' He darted back behind the curtains and said to Sister, 'Arrange for the urine output to be monitored.'

All the drama, tragedy, relief and suspense hung about them as Julian and Thea waited. The scene, familiar, nevertheless took to itself the atmosphere of an Impressionist painting; staff, patients, distressed relatives, part of a vast canvas.

'I'll telephone Lionel,' Julian said jerkily, and strode towards a kiosk, telling Lionel the situation and that Vicky was having all care and attention; but that until the blood tests came through and further examinations had been done, a diagnosis could not be made. Surgery had been ruled out for the time being.

At the other end of the line Lionel was secretly and guiltily grateful to be spared being there and having to wait about in Casualty, consoled by the knowledge that Julian and Thea would keep a watching brief and were, in any case, familiar with the whole procedure. It affronted him to reflect that Vicky would choose to be in a public ward rather than in some luxurious private room at a fashionable clinic, as he had wished. These reflections did not diminish the gnawing anxiety and dismay he felt; dismay he betrayed to Robert, who disliked his own inactivity.

'She's been drinking and smoking far more than usual,' said Lionel, as though the words were an extension of his thoughts. 'That cruise did her more harm than good. There'll have to be some changes around here, when she comes through this.' He paused and added, half-apologetically, 'I give way to her—spoil her . . .' He paused as if waiting for confirmation.

'I can understand it being very easy to spoil Vicky,' Robert commented honestly.

Back at the hospital Dr Gregory said to Julian a little later, 'The lab results reveal a haemoglobin of 8.5 grammes per 100 mls.' A blood transfusion was begun.

Thea watched Julian's face which was set into firm lines of control. They had exchanged only a few stilted words. From time to time they saw Vicky, whose expression was pleading and pathetic. She conveyed that so long as they were *there* within reach, even if the curtain separated them, she was satisfied.

'If you'd like to go home——?' Julian looked at Thea with understanding.

Thea had no illusions that her presence mattered to him; he was too absorbed with his patient, she thought, criticism implicit in the assessment. Doctor's didn't usually keep vigil, but his being there seemed natural, as though he were part of a family.

And there came the moment when there had been no further vomiting and Vicky was sedated with intravenous Valium. Julian and Thea watched her being wheeled away—pale, vulnerable and pathetic—nurses in attendance, as she was admitted to Maitland Medical Ward under the physicians who were 'on take', the admitting medical team for emergencies. The houseman Dr Walters, part of the medical firm which was also on take, clerked her in and contacted Dr Summers, the Medical Registrar, about setting up a CVP (central venous pressure) to monitor over-transfusion and further bleed. Dr Summers agreed it was necessary and immediately inserted the line into the subclavian vein just below the collarbone.

Julian and Thea went up in the lift to Maitland, which

Julian knew, along the wide corridors with their little information bays, signposted doors and strange quiet. Julian had a word with Dr Summers, standing at the entrance to the ward where he could see Vicky's bed nearby.

'She should have a good night,' Dr Summers said reassuringly, knowing Julian and having been put in the picture as to why he was there. Dr Summers was a tall, upright man in his early thirties, able and unassuming.

Julian and Thea walked back to the lifts; two nurses joined them. Thea felt she was living through some strange dream, until reality struck as they reached the hospital doors.

'We'll have to get them to call a taxi,' said Julian, and for the first time a wry expression touched his lips.

'Oh, of course,' said Thea, grateful for the mundane. 'No cars.' They returned to the hospital.

'I'll get two taxis,' Julian said without hesitation. 'One to take you home. I shall go back to The Drive and give Lionel the details. We shan't get a firm diagnosis until she's had more tests. Thank you for your support, Thea—it's been a great help.'

Did he, she asked herself rebelliously, realise just how closely he had associated himself with Vicky? Or how obvious he had made the familiarity of the doctor-patient relationship? In addition, came the critical thought, what had it to do with her?

Thea rang Julian early the following morning. He had just come out of the shower and there was a note of impatient urgency in his voice which changed to an, 'Ah—h——!'

'I wondered,' said Thea, 'if I should get in touch with

Lionel. Vicky will need toiletries taken in. Obviously she has friends, but I know the routine, and Rose will help.'

Julian said immediately, 'That's a splendid idea. Give Lionel a call. Vicky's had a good night, as Dr Summers predicted. I've spoken to Lionel.' Thea thought he was trying not to sound anxious.

'I shall be a little late in,' she warned him.

'We'll cope. Vicky will be grateful for your help. They'll let you see her, but she won't be allowed visitors in the ordinary way.'

Thea went to The Drive. Lionel, solemn-faced, greeted her with, 'I don't like this. Julian should get her transferred to Downlands (the Nuffield Clinic). Ridiculous,' he added, as though Thea understood what he meant.

'Vicky didn't want to be alone,' Thea told him. 'She'll have every attention.'

'Haven't even made a diagnosis,' he grumbled. 'Can't understand why Julian didn't pull strings——' He paused, abashed by Thea's steady scrutiny. 'I suppose,' he added quickly, 'he knew of her preferences——'

'As he's her doctor that's a foregone conclusion, but all he thought of last night was speed and the nature of the case. He's well known at St Stephen's, too.'

Lionel made a gruff sound. 'I suppose that's something. My wife has some very strange ideas. I sometimes think she despises luxury.'

Thea didn't mince matters.

'The only important thing is that nothing more could have been done no matter where she was. And they won't make a firm diagnosis until they've checked her thoroughly. What they may think, or suspect, isn't enough.' She felt impatient and irritated by his concentration on the social niceties and aspect. It would go against the grain for Lionel to visit his wife in a public ward when he could afford to pay ten times over for a private room. Basically, he was a snob, which was one thing she detested. And that snobbery took precedence over Vicky's wishes.

Rose Briggs had collected the things Thea listed. She was devoted to Vicky, who would sneak into the kitchen and perch on a chair, chatting about her early poverty, relieved to talk about it and what, then, had constituted luxuries. Lionel deplored this frankness and frowned on her doing anything that he could pay someone else to do. It was an aspect of his marriage that grated, but he knew that all his influence would not change her and that she would be far more comfortable among other patients than alone.

He looked faintly awkward.

'I'm sure you're right, Thea. It's just that I want the best for Vicky and I'm worried—desperately worried.' He added irrelevantly, 'At least I can give a generous donation to the hospital.' He wanted Thea's esteem. 'They're always needing some piece of new equipment . . . she will be all right? I can't get over the *shock*.'

Thea left him a few minutes later and went straight to the hospital, and into another world. Uniforms and white coats. Nurses, all seeming miraculously to have slim figures and attractive faces, encouraging smiles and measured steps. Snippets of conversation exchanged in passing: 'Old Mrs White wanted to be bathed in her nightdress and thought it was Christmas . . .', 'The new houseman is smashing', and 'Old Misery-guts Wilson is in a bloody mood'—intermittent exclamations coming from the domestic staff as they polished the floors until they shone like mirrors. The organised chaos of bodies being wheeled to theatre—the sensation for the dozy patients of being at sea. Endless cups of tea, coffee and other beverages . . . the rumble of food containers as they were pushed down endless corridors—music to some; relieving boredom for others; avidly received by the hungry. The sight of Sisters or nurses coming into the ward, a break in the long hours of waiting. Rows and rows of human beings in beds with wounds to be dressed, bedpans to be given, tablets to be taken, people in varying degrees of pain, discomfort; the terminal cases often the most cheerful, brave and optimistic.

Maitland was a small attractive ward, painted in cream and flower-filled. Large heavy windows let in the April sun which fell on neat lockers housing all personal belongings. Thea noticed the cards that adorned the ledges above each bed. 'To a dear friend' . . . 'Get Well'. They would, she knew, be counted and treasured.

'Thea,' Vicky whispered, light brightening her face for a second. 'All these tubes,' she added wretchedly, looking like a frail doll, with colourless cheeks and a sudden woebegone expression in her dark-rimmed eyes.

'I've brought your things,' Thea said gently, and proceeded to put them in the locker cupboard and drawer, then sat down in the armchair beside the bed, the curtains of which were pulled back. On Vicky's left there was a young dark-haired appendix case; no one on her right. Two patients opposite were absent, having their respective operations, while a 'spleen' and 'gall bladder' were further down the ward. She had not been in any condition to talk, but had heard the cheery exchanges without being part of the scene. The pain was easier, but she felt that she was living in some illusory world, isolated and alone.

'Thank you,' she murmured, and put out her free hand.

'Lionel will be in a little later.' Thea watched Vicky closely. There was no reaction to the fact.

'You and—and Julian'—Vicky could not utter the name without giving it significance—'were so good . . . last night.' She made a face. 'It was *horrible*!' she added with distaste.

Thea saw Staff Nurse O'Dell approaching and got to her feet. The ward rounds would be starting in a little while with the consultant physician, Dr Sloane, taking all particulars. Staff Nurse had already spoken to Thea and knew why she was there. She smiled and looked immaculate in her navy-and-white uniform, a favourite with patients and those who served under her.

'I'm just going,' said Thea.

Vicky could not stay the words. 'Julian? Is he—will he . . . be coming in?'

Staff and Thea's eyes met for a second, then looked down at the patient.

'Later, no doubt,' Thea said practically. The grapevine already had it that Dr Fraser had remained with Vicky Holford until she was admitted and that the husband had not been there.

Staff turned over her watch and looked at the time.

'Dr Sloane will be seeing you in about an hour,' she said encouragingly to Vicky.

Vicky nodded, her gaze on Thea. She looked as though she was going to say something and thought better of it, then she said, 'I'm so glad to be here . . . friendly; people around. Thank you for bringing my things. Julian won't arrange for me to be moved? He knows how I feel.' She gave a little weak sigh. 'Everyone is so kind.'

Staff smiled and smoothed the sheets with a friendly, almost protective gesture. There was something isolated and lonely about Mrs Holford that touched her, although she made it a rule never to get too involved with the patients.

Thea said a few more words and moved away, Staff with her. They walked down the ward together.

Thea made a point of mentioning Lionel. 'Mr Holford will be along a little later,' she explained. 'I suggested that he wasn't too early.'

'Splendid, although husbands have special rights, as you know . . . you work for Dr Fraser?' It was said with a degree of envy.

'Yes,' Thea replied with a smile. 'I trained at the Royal Sussex.'

'Dr Fraser's terrific,' came the somewhat irrelevant comment. 'Treats us . . . well, he lets us go first; little things . . . not easy to know, perhaps. All the more intriguing . . . ah, here comes Mrs Beck, back from theatre——' She moved swiftly towards the mobile bed which fitted into the stationary one. The swish of the curtains cut her off.

Back at Adelaide Crescent Julian came into Thea's room.

'How did you find her?' He spoke without any preliminary greeting.

Thea told him, finishing with, 'Until there's diagnosis there's little one can say.'

He stood uneasily, lowering his gaze.

'She asked if you were likely to be in.'

'Of course I shall go in. Later.'

'Which I said was likely.'

'A mind-reader.' It was a clipped sound.

Thea just stared at him without comment.

'Lionel,' he said abruptly, 'is being very trying about getting her into the clinic. I shall make damn sure she stays where she is.' There was a note of determination and near-possessiveness in his voice.

Thea retorted a trifle tartly, 'I'm sure you will.'

Julian's expression hardened.

In that moment she heard him saying, *'Will you have dinner at the Grand with me next week?'* It seemed important that the invitation should still be valid, even though it brought an element of confusion. Was this apparent interest in her, a subtle method of covering up a clandestine relationship with Vicky? Her body heated at the thought, first with a feeling of disillusionment, then fear professionally, followed by an almost personal sense of loss because, while there had never been any kind of friendly intimacy, he *was* a rather challengingly attractive bachelor.

She stood there in her white uniform, styled in the shape of a fitting coat-dress. It was edged with blue and had a blue belt which emphasised her slim waist. The sudden silence was awkward. He broke it by saying, wholly unexpectedly, 'How deeply do you think Vicky's miscarriage affected her?'

Thea stared at him unnervingly. She did not want to be drawn into any discussion since she could not be honest, and had no intention of indulging in subterfuge.

'You,' she said with disarming frankness, 'are her doctor, and should be able to answer that question far better than I.'

'But,' he countered unguardedly, 'she confides in you.'

'Even were that so, you wouldn't expect me to break that confidence,' she rebuked.

He looked annoyed.

'You seem determined to misunderstand me.'

A flame of irritation set her nerves tingling.

'Then may I suggest that Lionel, her *husband*, is the person to ask?' It was an overt criticism and he took it as such, anger darkening his eyes.

They faced each other stormily and he strode from the room.

In a matter of minutes Vicky had assumed a dangerous importance.

Enid put her head around the door.

'Ready? You've got a patient who looks ghastly— Miss Hardy.'

Thea's brows puckered. Brenda Hardy was the last person to look ill.

'Send her in,' Thea said anxiously. 'Probably something Dr Fraser will have to deal with.'

Brenda Hardy, normally a vital happy girl of twenty-two, auburn-haired, casually smart, seemed to have been stripped of all colour. Her face was pinched, her eyes large and hunted.

'Brenda!' Thea knew her on a friendly basis, as with most patients. 'What's *wrong*?'

'I'm not pregnant; I'm not ill, but I'm worried out of my mind.'

Thea relaxed a little; the pregnancy-abortion problem was all too familiar.

'Sit down and tell me about it,' she said gently. 'Dr Fraser is pretty good at solving problems and I can put him in the picture,' she added encouragingly.

Brenda sat down, slumped like a rag doll, and began, 'As you know, I'm engaged to Paul—and we've been engaged for six months. We're to be married in June. We've got the house we dreamed of, furnished it exactly to our taste——'

Suspense was building up because the facts didn't tie in with any worry.

Brenda's voice shook. 'The florist's shop is thriving and Paul's been made manager of the Craft Centre. It would seem that we're the luckiest couple——'

'And you're not?' Thea tensed.

Brenda looked down at her hands, wrung them in a gesture of desperation as she shook her head and then added, 'I've never bed-hopped. There's been only one other man, just before I met Paul eight months ago. It was a wild impulse at a party. I'd almost forgotten—' she gave a little cry and repeated the word, '*forgotten*. Since then, obviously, there's only been Paul, and we didn't sleep together to begin with. We didn't want to be a live-in *anything*—just an old-fashioned couple if you like, which sounds silly as I sit here saying it.'

'Not to me, but I don't see——'

There was a moment of heavy silence as drama built up.

'The man I slept with, Jeremy; I've just learned that he's dead——'

'But,' Thea put in, 'while that's sad, I don't see——'

There came a sudden piercing cry, '*He died of AIDS!* Don't you see? I could have it, couldn't I—*couldn't* I?' The agony of her expression seemed to turn her face to marble. 'What am I going to do?'

Thea asked gently, 'Are you absolutely sure of your facts?'

'Quite sure. I haven't seen him since that night, but friends of mine knew him well. They've been in South Africa just recently and on their return came to lunch. They brought his name up and spoke of the tragedy, knowing all the details. You see,' Brenda went on, her voice shaking, 'there's Paul; even in these few days I've tried to avoid any sexual contact and it looks as though I don't want him near me. Oh, we were quite honest with each other in the beginning; I told him there'd been someone else, just that once, and he told me that there'd never been anyone but me because no one had ever mattered. He's a very special understanding person and has never mentioned the subject again . . . I can't tell him about this. I just *can't*!'

'You'll have to,' Thea insisted, 'but first of all you must see Dr Fraser. Paul is also his patient. Dr Fraser will want a blood test.'

'And that will——'

'It will show if you have HIV infection—the virus.'

'Oh God!' Brenda said brokenly. 'What are the chances—what *hope*?'

'Always hope,' said Thea. 'Once——'

'You mean like pregnancy. Some girls conceive when they're virgins; others can sleep with lots of men and escape pregnancy altogether, even if they have children later on?'

'Exactly,' Thea agreed.

A groan escaped the pale shadow of the girl in the patients' chair.

'I could have it and have given it to Paul.' There was a note of dread in the utterance.

'Let's not think along those lines,' Thea suggested. 'I'll find out if by any chance Dr Fraser can see you now.'

Brenda put both hands immediately below her rib cage.

'I feel ghastly.' She pleaded, 'Would you explain to him first—tell him? My mouth is so dry, I'll never get the words out. And I'm terrified. It's Paul . . . to have to face *this* . . . If I could have the test and it proved negative—' She couldn't get any more words out.

Thea said kindly, 'I'll talk to Dr Fraser before you see him. Wait here. I won't keep you very long.'

Julian was free due to a cancellation, and saw Thea with an expression of surprise as she moved swiftly into his consulting room. The memory of the last words they had exchanged, and his abrupt exit, lay between them for an instant while they looked at each other with a certain antagonism, until she said briefly, 'Your patient Brenda Hardy. She wants me to put you in the picture before you see her.'

'Oh! Trouble?'

'Afraid so.' Thea didn't waste time. She gave a concise outline of the case. He listened intently, his only exclamation or interruption being his echoing of the word *AIDS*, with all its horrific implications.

When Thea had finished he said gravely, 'The first thing is a blood test, and Paul must be told.'

'Before we have the result?' It was a tentative question.

'A tricky point. If he's not told and it should be positive, her reluctance to have intercourse might very well precipitate a dangerous situation. An angry suspicious man,' he added bluntly, 'could be a danger to himself in the circumstances.'

Emotion gave his words significance, the subtle innuendo highlighting the situation.

'I have a duty to protect both patients,' he added, 'and it's essential that no risks are taken until they're given a clean bill of health.'

The enormity of the situation struck home as Thea realised that a positive result would automatically put Paul at risk. It was not merely the terror associated with the disease, but the effect on human relationships and permutations of tragedy.

'I see your point.' She sounded doubtful.

'Without agreeing with it,' Julian suggested a trifle sharply.

Thea knew, irrespective of the Hardy case, that his nerves were raw. Vicky lay like a ghost between them.

'Since Brenda has been honest about the isolated incident and isn't deceiving him about her actions——' She paused.

'Ah,' Julian put in, 'a secret blood test for AIDS? Where would that fit in? And the parents—both sets?'

'I know.' Thea's voice shook. She dared to say unguardedly, 'And suppose you were in Paul's position and were *told*?'

She saw him tense; his expression darken, while his eyes blazed.

'We're *not* discussing my personal reactions,' he retorted icily, 'or my affairs. Send the patient in.'

Thunder might have reverberated through the room, and at that moment Lionel was hurriedly admitted by an agitated Miss Jenkins murmuring, 'Mr Holford was——'

Lionel ignored her. It was enough that he wanted to see Julian who he had been told was with Thea.

He looked at Julian intently. 'I've just come from my

wife,' he said, somewhat aggrieved. 'She expected you would be in this morning. I want an eye kept on her. She's distressed——'

Thea had hurried to the door and glanced back. Julian was immediately alert, looking slightly awkward as he said, 'I shall be going when I've seen my next patient. I wanted a word with Dr Sloane and he won't have been on his rounds.'

'Red tape,' Lionel muttered. 'My only concern is Vicky.' His tone was warning.

Thea held her breath as she heard Julian say earnestly, 'So is mine.'

CHAPTER THREE

THEA lowered her head, then raised her eyes to meet Julian's as he spoke; their exchange of glances significant, for there was no harmony between them. Lionel got in a last few words. 'After all, I understand the patient's doctor is allowed to attend him, or her, automatically at St Stephen's.'

'Which,' agreed Julian, 'is true . . . but I must see my next case, Lionel.'

Thea still waited at the door. Lionel joined her. 'I'm sorry to have interrupted you,' he said in parting to Julian. 'Let me have a report later on.' He added, 'It isn't as though Vicky has a telephone and one could ring her.'

'At the moment she's in no fit state to be worried by calls!' Julian exclaimed.

Lionel's lower jaw jutted out; he looked aggressive. He was accustomed to being wholly in charge, his money the Open Sesame. He resented Julian's authority and discounted friendship.

'I'll send your patient in,' Thea said briskly.

'*Bring* her, please, Nurse. I'd like you to be here.'

Lionel and Thea left the room together, meeting Robert in the corridor outside. Robert was hurrying, but paused to enquire after Vicky, already having spoken to Lionel that morning after staying late at The Drive the previous night.

'How long do *you* think Vicky will be there?' Lionel

looked at Robert enquiringly, as though Robert's opinion was of the greater importance.

'Impossible to say until the trouble has been diagnosed.'

Lionel burst out, 'If I'd had my way——'

Robert had no patience to listen to the record being played yet again. 'Sorry, Lionel, I must rush.' With that, and a meaning glance at Thea, he made for the lift.

Brenda Hardy felt an overwhelming relief when Thea reappeared, as though, by some miracle, Thea could take away the agony gnawing at her; and when Thea said she was accompanying her, cried out, 'Oh, I'm so glad! I feel so lonely.'

The words struck a chill at Thea's heart and Julian's opinions seemed shattering.

They went into his room together. He came forward, shook Brenda Hardy's hand, steered her to the chair facing him across his desk and said gently, 'Nurse Craig has told me all the facts, Miss Hardy, and the most important thing is that you understand I'm here to help you no matter what may arise; and that I have only your welfare at heart. I'm not a judge, or a critic. It's important that you regard me as a friend.'

His deep attractive voice echoed in the heavy silence which Brenda broke by gasping, 'I can't tell Paul . . . I *can't*! I'd rather die.' She added, 'That isn't being dramatic—really it isn't; we've no secrets from each other in any way, but this is different——' She groped, her hand fluttering appealingly. Thea, with a glance at Julian, took it in a gesture of reassurance and compassion.

'And far more grave,' Julian told her. 'We can't gamble on your being free from infection, therefore Paul is at risk.'

'But,' Brenda pleaded, 'he has been ever since——'
She stumbled on, 'I mean, if we avoid intercourse——'
Again she broke off helplessly, knowing how her resistance to any physical demonstration had already created
problems, and that prolonged denial could precipitate a
crisis. She managed to explain this.

Julian went on quietly but impressively. 'Then you
already have evidence of the dangers in that situation,'
he warned. 'You're not in control of Paul's actions, and
frustration can be dangerous.' He looked at her intently.
'The truth is sometimes easier to live with than suspicion
and doubt. Unfortunately, because you can escape an
infection for years, it doesn't preclude your catching it in
an hour.'

Brenda cried desperately, 'What am I going to *do*?'

Thea looked at Julian, tacitly seeking permission to
make a suggestion as she said, 'If it were possible for
Brenda to go away for a short while——'

He followed the trend of her thoughts as he exclaimed, 'You mean until we get the result of the blood
test?'

Brenda shivered. 'Of course, there is *that*.' She added
appealingly, 'Will you do it?'

Julian nodded. 'Yes; but the sample will have to go to
the hospital for testing.' His voice held a note of reassurance as he added, '*Could* you get away while we await
the result?'

'How long will it be?'

'Four or five days.'

Brenda puckered her brows and then said, 'My grandmother hasn't been well and we're due to go to see her.
She and I are very close. I could get in touch with her
today and ask her to phone an SOS. As you know, my

parents, brother and I run the shop, and they could manage without me for a short while——' She caught at her breath. '"Short while" will be like a life sentence.' She went on disjointedly, 'Paul would approve of my going. Granny lives in Wimbledon and it's an easy run.' Her expression hardened. 'My mother will be relieved by my volunteering; she hasn't much time for Granny.' As Brenda spoke, her eyes were on Julian's face, watching every shade of his expression. 'I could leave this evening. Paul has a meeting and we weren't going to see each other anyway . . . Oh, Dr Fraser, can we do that? *Can* I go?'

Julian answered gently, 'Yes; yes, I'll agree to that.'

Thea prepared the syringe for the blood sample. There was drama in the simple routine. A life, possibly two, and certainly the happiness of both, lay in that innocent-looking phial of fluid.

Brenda's moment of release had passed. She sat so still that she might have been frozen into inactivity. Only her eyes, glancing from face to face, gave her life.

'I've read everything I could find about all this,' she said with a sudden simplicity that held all the poignancy of the situation. 'There's been enough written about it . . .' Her expression changed. 'I can't stay away longer than a week. I must *know*—' She caught at her breath as the horror flooded back. 'If I could have a definite appointment——'

Thea glanced at Julian.

'Better leave us your telephone number,' he said kindly. 'You mustn't be kept in suspense any longer than necessary. I'll do all I can to expedite matters.'

'Oh, God!' said Brenda, choked. 'Is it *real*?' She

rushed on, 'I'd want to see you before—before going home if—if it should be nasty.'

'We'll arrange that when I ring you,' he agreed.

She wrote down her grandmother's number on the pad Thea handed to her.

'I shall tell my granny,' she said simply. 'I tell her everything, so you can say who you are.' She looked at Thea and then at Julian.

'*I'll* ring,' Julian promised.

Tears rolled unchecked down Brenda's face.

'Thank you,' she said brokenly as Thea led her away and saw her out, returning to Julian who was standing very still, looking over the sea. The horizon was a sharp ominous line; the sky suddenly stormy.

'I was grateful for your support,' he said unexpectedly. 'We can only pray it's negative . . . Now I'm going to Vicky,' he added. 'Robert is taking over a couple of cases and I know you'll deal with the routine ones. I shall visit St Stephen's again this evening after surgery . . . I'd like you to come with me.' It was a statement uttered as a question.

'If that's what you wish.' Thea inclined her head.

Was that, she asked herself, his way of legitimising his visits? In view of Lionel's attitude, that did not make sense. But, she argued, Julian was not a man to think, or plan, just for today. He always had his sights on tomorrow.

Vicky waited for Dr Sloane the consultant physician to come on his ward round. She felt weak and near to tears. Ward Sister Lock, Nurse Gaynor and Staff Nurse O'Dell had all contributed to her comfort physically and mentally; now there was the silence of expectancy, each patient 'ready' to be seen and apprehensive about what they might be told.

Figures appeared at the entrance to the ward, Sister hovering. The man in the dark suit, Vicky decided correctly, was probably Dr Sloane, the other, in a white coat, probably his Registrar. They 'swam' slightly as she tried to concentrate, for she had no strength and was only allowed water and glucose by mouth.

'Good morning, Mrs Holford; I'm Dr Sloane,' he said, moving to the side of her bed.

Vicky looked up at him and liked what she saw—a round-faced, reassuring man in whom one could confide and intinctively trust. Having studied her chart, he sat down in the chair. 'I want to ask you a few questions.'

'May I ask you one?' Her voice was weak; she looked frail and appealing.

'Certainly.'

'Will I be sick any more? I don't mind the pain; I can bear pain, but *that*—' she screwed her face up into an expression of distaste—'*that*'s revolting!'

He didn't hesitate. 'We're here to make sure it doesn't happen again. You speak of pain——' He waited for her response.

'I've been having it after meals and in the night.'

'Two to three hours after meals?'

'Yes.'

'And between about one and three am at night?'

Vicky nodded, her gaze in his.

'Relieved by milk or any alkalines?'

Again she nodded, but this time went on half-apologetically, 'I've been smoking more than usual, and drinking more too. It was inevitable on the cruise.' She explained about her miscarriage and the holiday, and that she and Lionel had only just got back.

'Ah!' Now Dr Sloane had the picture and added, 'So Dr Fraser has only attended you for the miscarriage and knows nothing of this?'

'I'd arranged to see him professionally, but I wanted a few days to quieten down and—' Again she looked apologetic. 'I don't really like a quiet life.'

'I see.' A faint smile changed to a look of gravity. 'You'll have to adjust to one for a while, I'm afraid.' He studied her intently, aware of the shadow behind the hollow, dark-rimmed eyes. 'Have you any worries? Stress? The miscarriage——' His expression was in the nature of the question.

'I accepted it,' Vicky said evasively. 'As for stress—' a rather pathetic look came into her face— 'most of us have *something*.'

'Problems are better faced up to, and resolved,' he suggested on a helpful note.

'Some can't *be* resolved,' she said, betraying more than she intended, 'but,' she hastened, 'that's another story.' She recalled having uttered similar words to Thea.

At that moment she saw Julian come into the ward, have a word with Sister, and look towards her bed.

Dr Sloane noticed the transformation that took place as there came a little gasp. '*Julian?*' Vicky stopped, met Dr Sloane's somewhat surprised gaze, and explained, 'Dr Fraser is—is a family friend.' Emotion had exhausted her.

'And a good colleague of mine,' came the immediate reply.

Julian reached the bed, looking at Vicky and Harvey Sloane simultaneously.

'And how's our patient?' he asked.

'A typical history of epigastric pain,' Harvey Sloane said briefly.

'Ah!' Julian exclaimed, not surprised.

'What will you do to me next?' It was a weak, rather apprehensive question as Vicky looked from face to face. 'More tubes?'

'No,' Dr Sloane reassured her, 'if you behave; only a barium meal.' It was moderately urgent and he added, 'We'll arrange it with the consultant radiologist for tomorrow morning. You'll only be allowed glucose and water today and nothing by mouth after midnight tonight . . . Dr Fraser will fill in any details.' He turned to Sister who was waiting to accompany him to his next patient and, with a nod to Julian, saying, 'I'll have a word with you later,' he left, the other patients watching avidly.

Vicky took in every detail of Julian's appearance as he sat down, looking doubly attractive to her in that moment.

'I've wanted to see you,' she said, her voice low and weak, no matter how hard she tried to sound otherwise. There was a yearning in her eyes as she gazed at him in silent pleading. 'I caused so much——' The words trembled away.

'Only your getting well matters,' he told her gently. 'I ought not to have sent you away on that cruise, but there were so many reasons why I thought it was for the best——' He paused significantly.

'I hated it. I've been weak and foolish——' Vicky put out her hand and drew it back, aware that the eyes of the other patients were upon them, to say nothing of the girls who had just wheeled in the tea and coffee trolley. Men of Julian's calibre stood out even among the many attractive doctors who appeared on the wards.

Julian looked tense and ill at ease, while trying to appear relaxed. The sight of Vicky struck a poignant note in which thankfulness echoed because, thus far, she had come through it without surgery. The barium meal would provide an answer and it could be taken from there.

'Thea will accompany me this evening,' he said, to change the subject.

'I wondered if you'd be coming again,' she said, holding his gaze.

'Thea's been very helpful . . . I'm sorry I can't stay, Vicky.' He got to his feet as he spoke, and looked down at her. 'In any case you need rest and quiet . . . you're comfortable in here?'

'Very. There's a Mrs Redcliffe in the bed opposite —the pretty fair-haired lady with the lovely smile. She came and sat with me and was so sympathetic . . . Julian?' It was an appealing sound and her eyes met his with inescapable questioning. 'Have I anything— anything nasty wrong with me, do you think?'

'Of course not,' he insisted. 'Don't even begin to think like that. We'll know after tomorrow.'

'It's wonderful that you can come in as my doctor,' she said, holding his gaze.

'I *am* your doctor,' he reminded her, and looked away.

'I know, but——' Vicky stopped, warned by his expression. She not only felt ill from the effects of her attack, but ill with a yearning that was like a wound throbbing mercilessly. She had fought against her love for Julian from the moment she faced its reality and, in turn, believed it was reciprocated. She realised its dangers and that for him it could spell wreckage, the end of a career. Tacitly she accepted its liabilities, drawing comfort and strength from his sporadic betrayal of emotion, concern, and the desire that lay between them. It strengthened the bond, the ambiguity tantalising, the wild headstrong streak in her finding a challenge in the word '*forbidden*'. It was a secret nurtured and well kept, and she congratulated herself on the subtlety with which she had drawn him into the circle of friendship under Lionel's protection, his original acceptance of hospitality seeming miraculous. Her friendship with Thea had strengthened the tie and widened the circle, Robert's inclusion completing the picture.

'I want to have a word with Harvey Sloane,' Julian said swiftly. 'Ah, Sister—' as Sister appeared—'is Dr Sloane about?'

'He'll be in my office any minute now,' she replied.

Vicky watched Julian's tall figure pass by the beds and out of sight, and it was as though he were taking her heart with him. She closed her eyes as she lay propped up on the pillows, and as she drifted off to sleep, her last thought was that he would be back and that she would not mind Thea being with him.

Julian startled Thea later that day by saying abruptly, 'I shall get Robert to look after Vicky when this is all over. It isn't a gynaecological problem.' He added, 'And he's seen her from time to time, anyway.' There was a certain aggressiveness in his tone as though defying any challenge.

Thea emphasised, 'You specialise in gynaecology, but you *do* practice general medicine.'

'Less and less,' he insisted as though making the point was important.

Thea stared him out. 'Your patient will have a say in——' She paused, frozen by his near-threatening expression. A chill touched her. Was he showing discretion in the face of dangerous eventualities, or protecting himself against further folly, knowing that while the penalties for misconduct with a patient were retrospective, concealment might be possible if precautions were taken now? Of one thing she was certain: he was a disturbed and worried man, and not only on account of Vicky's health. She wondered what had transpired at the hospital that morning to add to his stress.

'Have you seen Lionel?' she asked abruptly.

There was an awkward pause before Julian replied, 'I telephoned him from the hospital, as a matter of fact. He had a word with Harvey Sloane—I thought that would pacify him. He wants everything done yesterday and sticks to the belief that there's no talent in the NHS. He's an intelligent man, but it's very difficult when you have to remind him that the consultant at the hospital is the same man as the man at his desk in Harley Street, his skill the same at either address.'

It stood out in sharp relief that Julian would never have become friendly with Lionel had he not been Vicky's husband. Every piece of the jigsaw fitted.

Thea said boldly, 'You still want me to come with you this evening?'

'Of course.' He made it sound the most natural thing. 'Vicky will be looking forward to seeing you. The day will drag, even though she's in no condition to enter into ward talk,' he added.

Thea smiled. 'I like the "ward talk"!'

'"Patients' chatter" might be a better description. Nothing like hospital to remove all inhibitions and make each person a confidante . . . you know that.'

Thea smiled reminiscently, hearing the laughter of recovering patients who were living in a strange carefree land, away from domestic responsibilities and, if they were honest, when out of pain enjoying the experience. Always talking of when they were going home, but feeling almost depressed at the moment of departure from that safe protected world.

He said abruptly and irrelevantly, 'We could have that meal at the Grand this evening. No question of our staying long at the hospital, and afterwards it's always an anti-climax somehow.' He added as though afraid of having conveyed the wrong impression along the lines of not wanting his own company after leaving Vicky, 'Don't misunderstand me if I admit that I don't want to be caught up with Lionel should he be around.'

Thea commented facetiously, 'That at least places me above him on the list!'

'I'll book a table for eight,' he said, ignoring the remark and taking her acceptance for granted.

Thea dared, 'Won't it look rather insensitive, after the drama of last night?'

Julian stiffened. 'I haven't forgotten, and I'm not neglecting my *duties*,' he emphasised, 'because I go out to dinner instead of having it in the restaurant by my flat.' He added indiscreetly, 'Vicky will understand.' There was a second of tense silence before he made some commonplace remark to detract from the significance of the observation.

Thea realised that she was viewing the situation from the angle of her own suspicions. In normal circumstances a doctor did not cancel any social pleasures because a friendly patient was ill. It could also be taken as preparing a defence in advance so far as Lionel was concerned, for, obviously, he had no idea of any involvement between Julian and Vicky. Thea questioned her own motives for accepting Julian's invitation in the circumstances, but his personality was so overpowering that she had not the will power to reject his offer. Also, his previous antagonism and criticism had left a scar that still smarted. She had no guarantee that he would not revert to the mood. Womanlike, she was intrigued by that which she resented and, in truth, feared. Whatever, she reflcted, one might think of Julian Fraser, one could not ignore him, or ever dismiss him from one's calculations.

She said smoothly, 'I'd like an opportunity to shower and change after we've been to the hospital.'

'So would I. If we get back to our respective flats about seven . . .'

'And be at the hospital soon after surgery finishes —around six if we're lucky.'

'A good plan. We'll each go in our own car . . . Ah, hello, Robert,' as Robert joined them, 'would you like to be on call this evening while I take Thea to the Grand?'

Hell! thought Robert. Wasn't it enough that he had Howard Flemming as a rival? Had he now to include Julian—the one person he had regarded as being out of the picture?

'What about Vicky?' Robert spoke shortly.

'We're going to see her beforehand.'

Robert looked suspicious. Something, somewhere, didn't ring true.

'I don't mind being on call,' he agreed.

'Then,' Julian said complacently, 'that's splendid. Everything has been taken care of at St Stephen's. I've talked to Harvey Sloane and they're doing a barium tomorrow.'

Thea's and Robert's gaze met: each had the same thought, that Julian's voice and attitude struck a false note concealing a far deeper anxiety.

'Thanks.' Julian looked at Thea and, to her utter astonishment, said, 'How would you like to visit Mrs Manfield? As you know, they're fine, but I said I'd look in, and she'd like to see you. I've got an ectopic miscarriage recovery on my hands.'

Thea kept back the words, 'If you think I'm capable,' knowing the remark would be petty. She accepted without comment. Robert raised his eyebrows and gave a little concealed smile as he flashed her a glance of congratulation. He said with sudden eagerness, 'And can I book you for next week? The Theatre Royal has got that new play—I forget the title—opening before it goes to the West End. I'd better get into the queue, or you'll be going with Howard!'

Thea didn't hesitate. 'I'd love that, and I'm not going with anyone. I've got a standing invitation from my father for the theatre, in case I might miss something. I enjoy an evening with him—he has such a zest for life.' She spoke as she was walking towards the door. 'I'll go to Mrs Manfield now. The appointments are pretty heavy later on . . .'

'Don't be long,' Robert called out. 'I like to know my patients have been vetted!'

'With Thea at the receiving end, we certainly are unlikely to miss anything,' Julian added.

The door closed and Robert shot a somewhat surprised look in Julian's direction.

'A complete *volte-face*, I must say,' he exclaimed grudgingly.

'Do I detect a note of disapproval? Rather odd in view of your previous criticism of my behaviour to Thea.'

'Suppose we say I find you a trifle difficult to understand these days.' Robert didn't deceive himself: he was jealous of Julian. Before, he had discounted even the possibility of Julian ever going beyond a purely professional relationship with Thea. Now, he argued to himself, taking her out to dinner: and after the drama of the previous evening too. It was the last thing, and Thea's acceptance added to his disquiet.

Julian's expression was inscrutable.

'That's better than if you could read me like the proverbial book.' His tone of voice closed the subject.

Julian and Thea met at the hospital that evening, Julian having come from an emergency asthma case. They parked expertly in the space allotted and went into the familiar building through the main entrance, then up by lift to Maitland Ward.

Ward Sister Lock, still on duty, smiled a greeting.

'Mrs Holford's asleep,' she said. 'Her husband has been and gone . . . she's slept most of the day, which is good . . . it's time for her to wake up.'

'We shan't stay long, Sister,' Julian promised.

They walked down the ward where more vases were filled with fresh flowers which stood on the bedtables, making it look like a conservatory. They smiled a little greeting to the patients who were alone, expectantly watching the entrance for the arrival of loved ones.

Vicky didn't stir as they arrived, but within a second or two opened her eyes, looked at Julian and murmured, '*Darling!*'

There was a moment of embarrassed, tense silence.

Thea's gaze darted to Julian's face. It was impassive and his voice, when he spoke, was gently correcting. 'It isn't *Lionel*,' he said admonishingly, but with a faint smile, and drew up a spare chair after Thea had sat down, her gaze intently upon Vicky, who now looked confused. She never used the endearment to Lionel and was anxious not to embarrass Julian, or incur his displeasure.

'I—I was dreaming,' she said drowsily. '. . . What time is it?'

'Six o'clock,' answered Julian, but Thea had an idea that his thoughts were elsewhere and the 'darling' had shaken him, his adroit twisting of the episode not standing fire. Thea had no illusions whatsoever but that the endearment was a natural but unguarded welcome for him, and a flame of anger flickered across her heart. The idea of being used as a blind was infuriating. She was stupid to have agreed to go out with him that evening and she regretted the impulsive decision.

Conversation soon ceased; the silence held all the awkwardness of hospital visits once the initial questions and answers had been exchanged. In Vicky's case, she hadn't the strength to do much talking. Julian looked at her chart, reassured that her temperature and pulse, respiration and blood pressure, had all improved, her frailty, nevertheless, a poignant reminder of her condition such a short while ago. Thea's thoughts matched his at that moment: it seemed years, instead of hours, since Vicky had collapsed.

'What,' Vicky asked in her quiet restricted voice, 'are you doing this evening?' She looked from face to face and the sudden silence was, to Thea, dramatic.

'Going to the Grand for a meal,' Julian replied naturally.

Thea heard Vicky's, 'Oh, I'm so glad!' with an element of surprise, for there was no deception in the remark. 'I wondered what you'd do.' She looked at Julian and held his gaze.

Thea heard the echo of Julian's words, *'Vicky will understand.'* How right he had been and, equally, Vicky might have been talking with the understanding possessiveness of a wife about a husband, that he should not be alone.

'Glucose and water can be very monotonous,' said Vicky, as a wave of weakness seemed to overwhelm her. 'I'm so glad you're here, Thea,' she added somewhat disjointedly. 'You're such a comfort.' Her eyes widened as she darted a glance at Julian and as though by virtue of some secret code, added, 'Lionel said how thoughtful you'd been in telephoning him. We're very grateful. He's having a meal with a business colleague tonight, so I told him not to come in again.' She looked at Julian, seeking silent approval for her tact in bringing Lionel into the picture. She might have been atoning for the cry of *'Darling!'* 'I'm not looking forward to the barium meal in the morning,' she went on rapidly. 'Will this drip still be in?' she asked.

'Yes,' Julian said quietly.

'And this?' She indicated the central venous line.

'That will have been removed.'

Vicky sighed. 'Thankful for small mercies . . . now you must go.' She looked from face to face as though giving them her blessing. 'I'm quite all right. I gave you a beastly time last night . . . have some champagne for me,' she added weakly.

'We'll wait until you're well again,' Julian said instantly.

She turned a loving gaze upon him. His words pleasing her.

Thea shivered, and felt she was being drawn into a dangerous web.

Julian and Thea went through the swing doors of the Grand Hotel and up the marble stairs to the reception lounge. An impressive commissionaire in black uniform, silver braid and top hat, respectfully acknowledged Julian's friendly greeting, while the glamorous girls on reception in their Air Force blue uniforms smiled, thinking Dr Fraser had an air about him that negatived most other men, and although he was not exactly a regular visitor, he was always noticed.

Thea took in the large reception hall with its colour scheme of blue and cream from which the imposing staircase rose, with a sweeping grandeur immediately facing them.

'Shall we go straight in?' said Julian in the tone of one who hoped she would agree.

Thea nodded approval, experiencing a wave of depression as she became aware of his distraction and the feeling that he recognised that their coming out to dinner was an error of judgment which he regretted. Vicky walked between them like a pale shadow.

The dining room was vast, colonnaded and elegant, with floor-to-ceiling windows draped in apricot striped material which toned with the pale red chairs and carpet. The tablecloths were deep pink and the napkins fan-shaped. Flowers completed the picture. There was an air of tranquillity, and the background music was peaceful and melodious. The head waiter, dressed in black uniform with tails and silver braid, greeted Julian as though he were the only customer in the room and showed them to a table that had a distant view of the sea.

Thea's feet sank into the deeply piled carpet and, in different circumstances, she would have looked forward to the evening.

'It's quite a time, Henri,' Julian said with forced gaiety, 'since I was here.' He paused and added, 'Nurse Craig and I have just come from a very sick patient and we're in the mood to have a choice made for us.' He looked at Thea as though the remark was perfectly natural, rather than incongruous since he assumed she shared his reactions.

'Ah!' Henri decided that the beautiful nurse was somewhat abashed by her escort's remark.

Thea smiled up at Henri and said, 'I'd like just one course.' She ignored the menu.

Julian appreciated her aplomb.

'Braised duckling with a garnish of fresh figs?' Henri suggested.

Thea looked approving. 'I'd like that.'

'Make it two, Henri.'

Henri spoke to the wine waiter who had been hovering discreetly. Julian looked at him and said simply and directly, 'Château Calon-Ségur.' He looked at Thea. 'And an aperitif?'

'A Tio Pepe,' she replied promptly.

'Two,' Julian repeated.

When they were alone, Thea said meaningly, 'You should have put this evening off. I feel awkward.' At that moment she was in no state to be discreet. A reluctant host was not the height of enjoyment.

He stared her out, not prepared to be intimidated.

'We shall both feel better when we've had something to eat,' he said smoothly, and went on, 'Amazing how magnificently they've restored this place . . . I looked after Henri's wife when she had her first child,' he added conversationally. 'I may not see him very often, but he's a damn good psychologist, which is the secret of his success. Knows when to talk and when not.'

'So I observed,' Thea commented, irritated by Julian's refusal to discuss his feelings, while not, in truth, expecting him to do so.

The sherries were brought and they relaxed slightly. It was useless, Thea argued, to expect him to discuss Vicky, or betray his reactions in any way. Obviously, the *'Darling!'* had to be accepted without significance. Womanlike, she resented the need to act as a fool, blind to the obvious. On the other hand, could she possibly expect him to confide in her, or make Vicky a subject of conversation beyond her immediate state of health?

Julian put his glass down, sighed, and she saw his shoulders drop as he relaxed.

She felt his gaze upon her as though he were seeing her for the first time and liking the picture she presented. She looked elegant in red and white, her hair loose and shining, her eyes vividly blue and inviting. The rounded firmness of her breasts was shaped beneath slender folds of material which emphasised her unusually small waist.

Her bare arms were smooth and the colour of honey.

'What,' he asked unexpectedly, 'do you enjoy in life—the little things, for instance?' His voice had changed and was low and encouraging, his expression enquiring.

'Little things?' she echoed a trifle breathlessly. 'They'd sound so trivial.' Her red lips parted into a wide smile. 'One that comes readily to mind . . . an extra hour in bed in the morning; going into the flat when Mrs Hobbs has been and there's a smell of furniture polish, with everything shining . . . a good book and the time to read it.' She paused, hesitated and then added steadily, 'And bathing, dressing and going out to dinner in the right circumstances and with the right man.' Her words came breathlessly and, she realised with embarrassment, involuntarily.

There was a second of electric silence which Julian broke by saying, 'And have you found him?'

Thea knew with a devastating suddenness that she had. And that he, Julian, was the man.

CHAPTER FOUR

THE SHOCK of discovery brought momentary panic and reduced Thea to silence. Julian's steady gaze was challenging and inescapable, and she felt the blood heating in her body as a new awareness of him awakened a desire, shattering and totally unexpected. *Julian*. She must be dreaming, influenced by the impressive romantic surroundings, and the fact that they were dining alone for the first time.

'Well?' he prompted with determination.

'I was speaking figuratively. I haven't found the right circumstances, I assure you.'

'You're being evasive.'

'And you're being persistent,' she countered.

'Intrigued,' he corrected, the atmosphere changing as he studied her with inescapable directness. The thought of Robert loomed somewhat alarmingly: he didn't want any complications in the practice, he told himself.

Thea was painfully aware of him and lowered her gaze, angry with herself for making such an indiscreet statement which was no more than an impulsive reaction, before reality struck to rob her of control. Her heart had quickened its beat and emotion brought confusion as she faced the prospect of the meal ahead, her nerves tingling, her thoughts chaotic. She heard the echo of his words, '*You'd no right to deliver the Manfield baby*.', and tried to cling to the memory to whip up anger which might counteract her vulnerability.

'Suppose you list a few things that *you* enjoy,' she suggested with a determined air. '*You* asked the question in the first place!'

He didn't hesitate. 'Being satisfied that a patient will recover——'

Thea felt a pang of jealousy. Vicky, of course.

'That's professional,' she countered.

'It can also be personal.' The words were spontaneous and he went on swiftly, 'An early morning swim——'

But the mood had changed and his words fell flat.

'I don't think you have anything grim to fear with Vicky,' said Thea, determined that he should know she was not blind to events.

His voice was sharp. 'I was speaking generally.'

'Let's say we've both been obtuse.'

They were on the edge of dissension; emotion, annoyance and frustration taking over from harmony. Obviously Julian's thoughts were with Vicky now; ironically, her own were with him. There was no spark with which to light a mutual enthusiasm, only the flame of dissension burned between them.

And then he said startlingly and unexpectedly, like a man who could not stand further apprehension, 'Your remark about Vicky . . . was it instinctive optimism?'

'Just instinct. The optimism was aimed at setting your mind at rest,' she added deliberately.

'I suppose there's an element of guilt about it where I'm concerned,' he admitted, adding, 'The fear that I'd overlooked the obvious.'

'That's ridiculous,' Thea said promptly and honestly. 'She's been away for two months.'

He finished his sherry.

'You're reassuring. Of course.'

'On the other hand, the mental and emotional state of a patient has to be taken into account. You were aware of that when you attended her at the time of her pregnancy and miscarriage.' Thea spoke with steady deliberation, her gaze unnerving.

Julian said hurriedly and dismissively, 'That's another matter.'

'If you say so.'

He frowned and said, 'It's dangerous to jump to conclusions. Miscarriages are a minefield.'

Thea resigned herself to the fact that his thoughts were at the hospital and that this dinner was in the nature of an escape. A bleak sensation stole over her and she resented the fact that now he had the power to make her unhappy. She was furious to be at the mercy of her emotions. His presence was disturbing, and mocked her previous *sangfroid*, awakening sharp desire which made his every movement significant and his gaze a powerful challenge to her self-control. Her thoughts raced: but for Vicky there might have been a tantalising hope of fulfilment. Her body heated at the possibility of lying in his arms, feeling the passion of his kiss. His very remoteness on occasion increased his fascination and made her wonder if her reactions to him had not been the herald of this surrender, this shattering awareness of being in love with him. Sensation followed sensation, her body responding to every erotic reaction—new and a little frightening.

'The greater the disappointment, the sooner another pregnancy occurs,' she said smoothly. 'Assuming there's a satisfactory medical history.'

'You're generalising.'

'Admittedly.' Thea could not particularise. 'I'm shocked that you're withdrawing from the case.'

Julian looked at her intently, his manner anxious, tentative.

'It isn't going to be as easy as I imagined.' The words slipped out.

Thea felt irritated by his confidence.

'Doctors don't usually abandon their patients without very good cause. It's not for me to question yours.'

His expression darkened. 'Mine is the belief that Robert is the better all-rounder. General medicine is his forte.'

'So,' she said, staring him out, 'you would still take care of her gynaecologically?'

Julian looked awkward. Then he said startlingly, 'Thea?'

She was conscious of the urgent note in his voice.

'Yes?' She spoke a little breathlessly.

'Vicky needs a friend—a woman who would understand her. Beneath all the gaiety there's uncertainty, even sadness. I can't help,' he admitted.

Thea tensed. 'Are you suggesting that I can? We're friendly already.'

'I'd like to feel Vicky had a trustworthy confidante.'

Thea wanted to snap, 'She has a husband—or have you forgotten, the wish being father to the thought?' But instead, with rigid control, she said, 'I'm prepared to fit into the picture in whatever way you wish.'

She saw a flash of relief pass over his features and a faint sigh escaped him as though a burden had been lifted.

'Thank you,' he said quietly, lost to the incongruity of the situation. Vicky was a married woman and his patient, yet he had no compunction about showing a dangerous interest in her welfare, or confiding his anxiety. Was it, Thea asked herself, because in an emergency he knew he could rely on her, Thea's, loyalty? Or had he it in mind to use her, as she had already suspected, as a blind and a cover-up? She shivered at the prospect, knowing that at the moment it was not in her to deny him help in no matter what direction. She bitterly regretted becoming involved with Vicky in the first place.

Julian lost his tense attitude, looked around him and back to meet Thea's direct gaze. Their meal was served and he ate it swiftly, like all doctors, who never know if they are going to be lucky enough to finish it, and the occasion didn't change the habit. Conversation became general, and as Thea sat there, she reminded herself that nothing would ever be the same again after this evening with its moment of revelation about her feelings. She tried to overcome the selfconsciousness of emotion, to think of something to say in the little awkward silences that punctuated the discussions. By the time coffee was served her nerves were like taut violin strings, and Julian asked directly, 'Is something troubling you?'

Colour rose in her cheeks. She sipped her coffee to gain time before saying, 'Nothing . . . Why?'

'You seem strained . . . miles away.'

'Enjoying the meal and the surroundings,' she countered lamely.

'I'm afraid I'm not as entertaining as my cousin.' It was a rueful sound.

'More on your mind, perhaps,' said Thea deliberately, a faint edge to her voice.

But he was lost to the implication and nodded, as

though he had already ceased to be interested in the remarks. She had the bleak feeling that the evening had been a failure, apart from the agreement that concerned Vicky. It was as though, having got her assurance on the friendship issue, Julian had no further involvement. She dared not challenge him because desire robbed her of control and argument would be dangerous.

She refused more coffee.

'You're tired,' he said quietly.

Thea gave a little mirthless laugh.

'And look ninety!'

'At the moment I think it would be difficult for me to say the right thing,' he retorted, the old flame of contention flaring.

'It hasn't been a restful twenty-four hours,' she reminded him.

'My God, it hasn't!' he agreed fervently. He summoned the waiter and signed the bill. There was a finality about it that hurt her. She didn't want a rift; she wanted harmony, but didn't know how to achieve it. Her love for him was overpowering, and as they finally reached the exit and went down the steps, he put a hand against her elbow and his touch was like an electric shock. When they reached the pavement, they stood looking out over the sea where the afterglow spanned it like a rainbow. There was a soft sensuous breeze that fanned their cheeks as they moved to Thea's car parked nearby. Julian was walking.

Despite the conflict, Thea didn't want the evening to end. She hadn't made the most of it because she was too torn by the love that tormented her as they reached her car and she unlocked the door, which he then opened for her. If only she could return with him to his flat, feel the thrill and excitement of his arms around her, his lips on hers. Involuntarily her gaze went to his and, to her amazement, he leaned forward and kissed her forehead.

'Thank you for your help and understanding,' he murmured softly.

Passion and disappointment mingled as, trembling, she got swiftly into the car. Julian closed the door and she wound down the window, flashing him a hard little smile as she drove swiftly away.

'Now,' Nurse Gaynor said to Vicky the following morning, 'you're going for a ride to the X-ray department, for your barium meal.'

All the blood necessary had been given and the central venous pressure line had been removed.

'Can't I get rid of this drip?' Vicky pleaded.

'Not yet.' Nurse Gaynor added, 'It's only a normal saline solution running in slowly to keep the line open.'

'You're very pretty,' Vicky exclaimed. 'And so good to me.'

'You're a good patient, and you must be very empty. Glucose and water are excellent, but——'

'I don't mind about the food. I don't mind anything as long as I'm not sick.'

Nurse Gaynor smiled. The two most common things she heard from patients of varying ages were that, after bedpans, they hated having to remove their false teeth and loathed being sick.

'I told you your husband rang . . .'

'Yes.' Vicky's heart quickened its beat. Julian hadn't rung.

'And Dr Fraser.' Nurse Gaynor added swiftly, 'He'll be in later.' She noticed the flush that crept up to Vicky's cheeks. Another patient, she thought, with an inward chuckle, with a crush on her doctor!

Vicky was wheeled to the X-ray department with the drip still running, and received by the radiologist, Dr Carter, a slim attractive man in his late thirties who smiled encouragingly. He explained the examination, finishing with, 'And do you suffer from glaucoma— eyes——?' he added.

'I know,' she assured him. 'But no, I haven't got glaucoma.' She looked wonderingly around the room, which seemed to be full of machinery of varying shapes, another doctor in a white coat, plus a nurse who stood beside her. Having been given granules and a special solution to drink which produced gas in the stomach, she was then injected intravenously with Buscopan to paralyse the stomach for about twenty minutes.

Vicky swallowed the barium when instructed, hating the raspberry-flavoured substance, which was thick and cloying; then stood, and lay, as directed, on the X-ray screening couch.

The procedure was new to her, and during the examination Dr Carter viewed the television monitor and took spot films as required.

'I think,' he said quietly to her, 'I've found a duodenal ulcer, but I'll just check the films.'

Vicky was not alarmed, because she had suspected the trouble lay in that direction. The diagnosis was confirmed. A certain relief came with the knowledge because the word 'cancer' had insinuated itself into her thoughts on many occasions in recent weeks, but her mental and emotional condition had been such that she could not sustain any belief for long. The deep gnawing pain intermittently frightened her, and she did not underestimate the folly of keeping the condition to herself.

She was thankful, finally, to get back into bed, even the ward seeming welcoming, the warm April day allowing the windows to be open. One of the patients had been transferred to Intensive Care; another had gone home and a third was in the operating theatre. Mrs Redcliffe came and sat down beside her. She was quiet, but concerned and enquiring.

'A duodenal ulcer,' Vicky told her. 'I'm thankful,' she added, her voice weak and her stomach churning after the barium, which made her feel slightly nauseated. She liked Mrs Redcliffe's bright sympathetic eyes and pretty face, framed with fair naturally curly hair. She could imagine her being fun and a source of strength to the other patients.

'That's been my trouble . . . been in four days; going home on Saturday. I mustn't tire you . . . here comes Staff.' She patted Vicky's hand and went slowly away to her bed opposite.

It was, Vicky thought, *contact*. There was a curious fellow feeling, almost as though Mrs Redcliffe were a relative; the bond of illness and being in hospital drawing them close, so that a few words sufficed. Vicky wished she had the strength to laugh.

Lionel and Julian arrived together. Vicky's heart sank. Julian had already had a word with Sister and knew the result, which he had suspected while not wishing to be too confident. There were so many complaints far worse to be feared.

Lionel looked awkward. His kiss was light, and he sat down on the edge of the chair, grateful for Julian's presence.

'I want to see you looking better,' he said absurdly, the remark aimed in criticism at the treatment being given. He turned to Julian, who had done no more than greet Vicky and remained standing by the bed, not intending to stay.

'All being well she should be home in five days from now,' Julian told him. 'A little later today the Medical Registrar will convey the facts to Dr Sloane and they'll decide on treatment . . . you'll forgive me if I rush away? I just wanted to know the result of the barium——'

'I'd like you to see her again this evening,' Lionel insisted. 'If you're not satisfied——'

'I am satisfied,' Julian assured him, hiding his irritation.

Vicky looked agitated. 'Please don't fuss, Lionel. I couldn't have more done. They've been checking me . . . I just want *peace*!'

Julian said, an authoritative note in his voice as he addressed Lionel, 'It's essential that Vicky has no strain or worry of any kind.'

Vicky's voice was weak and broken. 'I couldn't be any better looked after. Julian . . . knows.'

Lionel felt out of his depth as he agreed, 'Very well . . . very well . . . I'm only thinking of you. There'll be some flowers a little later——'

Vicky didn't want flowers; she wanted him to go so that she could have even a few seconds with Julian alone . . . the pain would ease then and she'd feel better. She looked at Julian—a swift flashing appeal. 'I want to ask you——'

Lionel got up. 'I'll let you discuss things with your doctor,' he said, 'and be back about five.' He kissed Vicky's forehead and went briskly and thankfully from the ward, not looking to right or left, and passing the nurses without a smile.

'Oh, Julian,' Vicky said piteously, 'he upsets me, and I thought you were going . . . I feel awful, but I *am* better; I mean, I shall be well again——'

'Provided you do as you're told.'

She held his gaze.

'You know I'll do anything—anything *you* say——'

'Then,' Julian told her, 'rest so that you'll get better quickly.'

She looked at him, her eyes glistening. 'I love you,' she said in a whisper.

Staff Nurse O'Dell didn't hear the words, but she saw the half fear, half embarrassment on Julian's face and felt the tension in the atmosphere. There was something about this case, she thought sagely, that was outside the patient-doctor crush, and the word that came to mind as she saw Julian's retreating figure was 'guilt' . . .

Later that afternoon it was decided to take down the intravenous drip and start Vicky on Tagamet—green tablets—while still checking her haemoglobin, the red chemical contained in the red blood corpuscles, at regular intervals.

Vicky's voice had a little more strength in it as she said, 'It's lovely to get rid of that drip . . . Am I still bleeding? I don't like to ask the doctors a lot of questions.'

'Occult blood has been detected by laboratory tests,' Sister told her without hesitation, 'and is still passing through your bowel; but eventually your faeces will become negative and you'll no longer be bleeding.'

Vicky gave a little sigh. 'How you can bear to cope with all you do!' she said appreciatively. 'Nurses are marvellous. How long before I'm back to normal?'

'About ten weeks. No smoking and definitely no alcohol.'

'Dr Sloane emphasised that.' Vicky sighed again. 'But I *shall* be out of hospital in about five days?' There was a note of urgency in her voice.

'Yes.'

'Dr Fraser said I should be.' Vicky liked mentioning Julian's name and her pulse quickened. She lowered her gaze and looked a little selfconscious. 'The barium stuff has churned me up, but the rats aren't gnawing me so much.'

Sister knew what she meant. Ulcer pain was often thus described.

'Everything is so strange . . . is it still Friday?' asked Vicky.

'Yes; and you've talked enough. Later on you can have some milk. A bland diet.'

'I like savoury things.' The words were muffled. Vicky closed her eyes.

Sister studied her as she slept, realizing how beautiful she was. She couldn't say she liked *Mr* Holford, she thought irrelevantly, which was the general impression among the nursing staff; also that Mrs Holford herself showed no enthusiasm for him either. At that moment Nurse Gaynor appeared with a basket of magnificent red roses.

Vicky opened her eyes and surveyed them, aware of the little murmur of appreciation among the other patients. She looked at the card handed to her, said, 'They're very beautiful . . .' and drifted off to sleep, aware of an aching sense of loss because they could not be from Julian and were, in fact, from Lionel.

Thea passed on a bronchial patient to Robert, made an appointment for a blood pressure check, an injection and ear syringing, and decided that she had time to snatch a cup of coffee which Enid always produced miraculously; but the intercom went and Julian said, 'Can you spare a few minutes?' His voice was urgent.

'On my way,' she said, and made for the lift, reaching his consulting room somewhat apprehensively. Since the evening at the Grand, Julian had been polite but subdued, as though he were living on a different plane.

He got up from his desk as she entered, grave, tense.

'I've just been on to the Southern,' he said swiftly.

'Brenda Hardy!' Thea cried.

'It was positive.' The words came like a death sentence.

'Oh God, no!' Thea caught at her breath and sat down weakly in the nearest chair while Julian returned to his desk. He held his hands up to his temples.

'At this moment I hate being a doctor.'

The sudden silence was broken only by muted traffic, its very normality mocking the tragedy locked within the room.

'I've got to ring her—tell her.' For a second the power, authority and control demanded by his profession deserted him.

'Oh, Julian!' Thea's voice broke.

The sound of his name, the plea implicit in it, brought them back to cold brutal facts.

'Now,' he said, his manner changing, 'the question is how to deal with it—protect Paul.'

Thea said with dread, 'If he's not already infected.'

Julian nodded. 'As you say.' He got up from his desk and, as always in moments of conflict, looked out across the sea. It was an angry sea, with dark clouds reflecting ominous patterns on the grey-green water that swirled vengefully to the beach, dashing against the groyne and rising into the air like a windswept Niagara.

Thea watched him, her love seeming a tangible element between them, his compassion a bond.

'I can't put it off,' he said half to himself, and held her gaze. 'This is a problem we have to deal with for the first time. A new and terrifying disease that can't be swept under the carpet, or dealt with by an antibiotic. AZT is merely a straw in the wind, and we know it will be years before there's an antidote. I feel absolutely powerless, without even the hope of a prognosis.'

Thea took in every detail of his fine figure; the clean-cut features, the glow of health. She loved him; it was heaven and hell; an all-pervading experience. Could she still do so if *he* had AIDS? A shudder went over her, and although the day was warm, she was icy. They lapsed into silence because there were no answers and no hope.

Julian took out his private diary, repeated a telephone number and lifted the receiver. His eyes met Thea's before he dialled. She stayed.

A second later he said, 'Could I speak to Miss Brenda Hardy . . . Dr Fraser. Ah, Miss Hardy. Yes. I'm afraid it's positive . . . will you come to see me on your way back?'

'About three?' The voice was broken and doom-laden.

'I'll expect you then.' He spoke gently.

Tears glistened in Thea's eyes.

'Make sure you're about when she arrives,' Julian said earnestly as he replaced the receiver. 'And get Miss Jenkins to manoeuvre things so that I'm free then.'

'I'll see to it.'

'I'd like you to be here with her. No one can imagine her desperation, or the agony of mind.'

Thea nodded. She couldn't speak.

Brenda Hardy arrived promptly. She looked as though she had shrunk to half her size, and her face was like parchment. When she saw Thea she gasped, 'Oh, I'm so glad it's you . . . you *know*?'

'Yes,' Thea replied. 'I'm so *sorry* . . . the words are totally inadequate.'

'You're not shrinking from me.' It was a quiet but surprised sound. 'Thank you.'

Thea could not think beyond compassion. Here was an innocent victim, guilty only of a single act, yet because of those few moments she now had a death sentence and was cursed for her remaining years.

Thea took her arm, led her to the lift, and to Julian who held out his hand and said quietly, 'I'm so sorry—so sorry.' He didn't know what he had expected from this young and vulnerable girl; what reactions. Hysteria, shock? He had no yardstick, no precedent. This was his first contact with the virus, and he prayed it might be the last, while knowing it to be a forlorn hope.

'I've been *through* the hell,' came the unexpected reply. 'Waiting, suspense, fear—they're even worse than the agony of knowing. There are decisions to be made now.'

'I must see Paul.' Julian spoke gravely.

Brenda added, 'And give him a test.'

There was a second of silence as she sat down and

faced Julian across his desk. Thea stood beside her protectively.

'Yes . . .'

'*I* shall tell him,' Brenda said firmly. 'I've realised in these past days that, in the end, the one thing a human being must have in whatever the circumstances, is courage. Besides,' she said with a slight lift of her head, 'Paul would expect it of me. I can at least keep his *respect*.'

Thea swallowed hard. This quiet acceptance was even harder to witness than wild hysterical anguish. It was as though Brenda Hardy had come to terms with the tragedy during the intervening days and accepted the death sentence.

Julian could only say, 'I'm ready to do anything that will be helpful. But if you've decided to tell him yourself——'

'Oh God!' came the sudden, terrified cry. 'I've refused to think of *his* being . . . I talk of courage——' she shook her head and choked back the tears, 'but for him to be—be condemned——' She put out her hands in pathetic appeal.

Julian soothed, 'Let's not anticipate the worst.' He thought hopelessly that it was like fighting a vicious enemy in the dark, not knowing where, or when, it would strike. All his professional knowledge, everything for which he had been trained, slid into an abyss of ignorance that petrified him, mocking all previous experience.

'And there's my parents—his parents.' It was a low dread sound. Brenda shuddered with distaste. 'I feel like a leper already.' She looked piteously from face to face. 'Oh God,' she cried, 'help me!'

Julian's voice was gentle, but firm. 'We've got to take

this step by step. It might be advisable if *I* saw your parents, put them in the picture.'

Brenda shuddered, the thought of her mother's reaction sapping every scrap of her courage. She was a hard woman, strict and devoid of compassion. She grasped Julian's offer with thankfulness.

'My father and brother!' she exclaimed, and stopped. 'How can *anyone* take it, except with horror? If I feel it about *myself*, what can I hope for from others?'

Thea took her hand.

The room was filled with a silence that seemed threatening. Brenda went over in her mind all she had read so avidly about the virus. *An incubation period between nine months and six years. Half the sufferers die within a year of diagnosis, and most are dead within four years. Not transmitted by touch, drinking from the same cup, shaking hands. Avoid anything that might have infected blood on it.* She and Paul had talked about it, proud of their own fidelity; vowing never to be unfaithful.

'*Paul!*' The name escaped her lips in a suppressed shriek as though someone had struck her an unexpected blow. Agitation took the place of calm as she cried, 'I must see him; tell him. Oh, Dr Fraser,' she rushed on, 'I'm so sorry to burden you with this, take up your time——' She got to her feet, swaying before Thea steadied her by putting an arm around her shoulder.

'What time are your parents most likely to be in this evening?' Julian asked supportively.

Her eyes, wide, scared, met his.

'Six-thirty,' she told him. 'The shop is shut and cleared up. They work afterwards, but——' Her voice faltered. 'I shall have seen Paul.' She became disorientated and spoke disjointedly. 'My father has a whisky then . . . I shall be in the house. Paul won't want to see me for long . . .' A faraway look came into her eyes and she moved mechanically to the door. 'Thank you, Dr Fraser.'

'I shall see you this evening,' he assured her confidently, '*with* your parents once they know the facts.'

She stared at him almost vacantly and nodded. Thea accompanied her out of the building and then went back to Julian.

'I felt so damned *inadequate*,' he exclaimed bitterly.

'You've done all you can—seeing the parents——'

'I must admit I dread that. I dread the *mother's* attitude.' The ringing of the private line made them both jump. He answered it immediately, his voice delighted. 'Vicky, you're home!' He added guardedly, 'No,' adding, 'Thea's with me . . . Later.'

Thea flashed him a cynical meaning glance and hurried from the room. It was obvious that Vicky had asked if he was alone. A sensation of anger, suspicion and jealousy quickened her heartbeat. She went down to her office where Enid awaited her. 'Your Mrs Pearce has just arrived and is putting on her voice of frailty,' Enid told her.

Thea groaned. Without any complaint, Mrs Pearce was an unhappy woman, and conjured up various ailments to attract attention, wanting desperately to get to see Julian, while not having the nerve to demand to do so once Thea had found that her blood pressure, pulse and respiration were normal.

The juxtaposition of Brenda's tragedy and this self-centred woman of forty-five made Thea greet her with no more than politeness.

'You see, Nurse,' she began without any preliminaries, 'I'm not well enough to go to my niece's
wedding.'

Thea looked at her case notes.

'I checked you out three weeks ago, Mrs Pearce.
You've been to me regularly and there's nothing wrong,
no symptoms of any kind. Your weight is normal. In fact
you're a very healthy woman.' She gave her a steady
inescapable stare. 'You don't want to go to the wedding,
and you need an excuse,' she added firmly. 'I can't give
you one.'

Mrs Pearce shrieked, 'Really! How dare you say such
a thing? I'll report you to Dr Fraser!' Her unpleasant,
ill-tempered face seemed to lengthen, the thin lips shut
in a hard accusing expression. 'You're not fit to have this
job!' She scrambled to her feet and made for the door,
bumping into Julian. 'Ah, Dr Fraser, the very man I
wanted to see . . . that nurse of yours; she's rude and
inefficient, and if I don't get some satisfaction I shall
report the case to the GMC . . . I'm a patient, and I
don't come here to be told there's nothing wrong with
me!'

Julian couldn't restrain himself from saying, 'Then if
there's nothing wrong with you, Mrs Pearce, I congratu-
late you. I have every confidence in Nurse Craig's
ability.'

'And I don't come here to be fobbed off by the
practice nurse! I've wanted to see you——'

'I'm available, Mrs Pearce—by appointment.'

'It's too late now,' she snapped. 'This is the last time I
shall come here; but you'll be hearing from me; oh yes,
you'll be hearing from me!' With that she bounced
towards the front door.

Julian went into Thea's office. Complaints were the last things he wanted to have levelled at the practice, particularly when made by a spiteful, frustrated woman.

'You heard all that,' he said somewhat sternly.

'She's impossible! A thoroughly fit woman who wants a medical excuse to enable her to get out of doing anything she dislikes.' Thea made a growling sound. 'If she stubbed her toe she'd call for an ambulance, or get out the Dettol and bandage it!'

Julian didn't smile, and tension mounted between them.

'And you think that's normal?' he enquired.

'Normal? She wouldn't know the meaning of the word,' Thea said disgustedly. 'A raging hypochondriac.' Something in his expression froze her, awakening fear.

'That being so, she needs help.'

She stared at him aghast.

'You don't mean you're in *sympathy* with her and that I'm wrong because I don't invent ailments to pacify her?'

'No; that you allow *me* to decide if she needs psychiatric help.'

The passion of her love for him mingled with anger, resentment and a feeling of injustice, so that she rapped out, 'So we're back to the Manfield baby!'

Julian said coldly, 'We're not "back" to anything; we're dealing with a specific case. So! Patients like that are pretty hard to take, but they're our *patients* and we're not their judges. Can you imagine what it must be like to live with someone like that?'

'Yes,' said Thea furiously. 'Hell!'

'Exactly. She has a husband and a couple of children. If we help her, we help them.'

Thea felt stubborn and difficult, her love for him raged

and whipped up the folly of argument as an outlet. 'We've enough sick patients to consider without——'

'Don't be so damned unreasonable!' Julian exclaimed, voice raised.

They were standing close to each other, emotion rising like a storm. Eyes met eyes, fury darkening them, and before Thea could move he had put his arms round her and kissed her roughly on the lips.

Desire flooded through her body and she tensed against surrender in case she betrayed her feelings. But suddenly, harshly, he released her so that she staggered slightly, colour rising to her cheeks.

'*I*'ll deal with Mrs Pearce,' he said with finality, and strode out of the office.

CHAPTER FIVE

THEA tried to control herself, to escape from the feeling that the kiss had been an outrage instead of a compliment, and his only way of expressing the annoyance he felt. There had been no tenderness, only violence. A sick misery stole over her and a weight seemed to have lodged beneath her rib cage, bringing an aching sense of loss. She cursed Mrs Pearce and shrank from his defence of her; yet wasn't he living up to the highest traditions of his profession in refusing to allow personal prejudice to cloud his judgment? He *had* defended her, Thea, against attack, and she clutched at that little ray of hope. In different circumstances she might have had her usual patience in dealing with the patient, but coming immediately after the drama of Brenda and the call from Vicky, her mood was intolerant. That in itself, and in her job, was inexcusable.

Enid said, 'Nurse, are you all right?'

Thea sat down at her desk, struggling to compose herself; to forget the pressure of Julian's lips fiercely on her own, the warmth of his mouth in that swift penetration. It had been so sudden, so totally unexpected and inexplicable.

'Better in health than in temper.'

'Dr Fraser's gone out as though there was a fire. His next patient is due in five minutes . . . yours has just arrived.'

Thea sighed and looked down at her notes.

'Mrs Metcalf . . . send her in.'

Enid decided that Nurse Craig looked definitely odd. As she said to Miss Jenkins, 'If you ask me, Dr Fraser and Nurse Craig have had words.'

'That,' said Miss Jenkins firmly, 'is their business.'

'He's just come back.' Enid heard the front door close.

Julian paused at Miss Jenkins' door and addressed her and Enid.

'I'm ready for the next patient.'

'Miss Newbury,' Enid said.

'Your last,' put in Miss Jenkins, looking at him for a second and then lowering her gaze.

'Thank God!' He spoke with friendly gruffness.

'I've never heard him say that before,' Enid declared as he left them. 'He certainly doesn't look his calm collected self. Fascinating man—you never know what he's thinking.'

Miss Jenkins didn't speak.

Thea saw Mrs Metcalf, who was in a state of euphoria.

'I'm pregnant! Pregnant,' she repeated with delight. She was twenty, had been married two years and was obviously particularly happy.

Thea expressed her congratulations, adding, 'It's always a joy when the baby is wanted.'

'Andrew's so thrilled—it's terrific!' came the jubilant exclamation.

Thea thought she'd never seen Fiona Metcalf look so beautiful, with her dark shining hair and creamy skin; eyes bright as stars—soft brown eyes that reflected every mood. 'I have to stop him buying toys already . . . can I see Dr Fraser? I mean make an appointment?'

'Miss Jenkins will attend to that,' Thea assured her.

'I'll just take your blood pressure—how far?'

'I've missed two periods, but I don't feel sick at all. I had one little faint turn, and my breasts are very tender.'

'And everything's normal,' said Thea when she had completed the routine. 'You look a splendid advertisement for pregnancy, and from what you say, it's more than likely . . . One minute . . .' She switched down the intercom and spoke to Miss Jenkins. An appointment was made for Friday of that week.

'Dr Fraser looked after me when I had 'flu . . .' A significant gleam came into Mrs Metcalf's eyes. 'He's dishy, isn't he? Terribly attractive.'

Thea struggled to keep the colour from her cheeks and be cool and impersonal. Such a short while ago she had been in his arms.

'Both Dr Fraser and Dr Robert are very popular,' she commented discreetly.

'But Dr Fraser is the gynaecologist.'

'Yes.' Thea added, 'Although Dr Robert takes quite a few midders.' She was grateful for a simple case to relieve the tension and showed the patient out, bumping into Robert as she returned to her office.

'The theatre,' he said without preliminaries. 'Have a look in your diary.' He followed her into her office. 'Next Wednesday?'

'A week tomorrow,' she agreed, finding the right page in her diary. 'Yes.' She didn't add that she was having dinner with Howard Flemming on the Tuesday.

Robert studied her. 'You don't sound very enthusiastic. Something wrong?' He stared at her searchingly. 'You've got that "God help me" look about you. Julian been upsetting you?' The wish was father to the thought.

'Just patients,' she said evasively.

'Vicky's out of hospital, I understand. I'm on call this evening while Julian sees her.'

'She's done very well . . . I must ring her.' Thea stopped, remembering Julian's appointment with the Hardys at six-thirty. He *couldn't* have forgotten *that* in his eagerness to visit Vicky. She asked a trifle anxiously, 'What time are you on call, by the way?'

'From six-fifteen.' He looked puzzled; Thea was never inquisitive. 'Julian had a special visit to make. He wanted to discuss it, but there wasn't time.'

'Ah,' Thea exclaimed, satisfied. 'So he hasn't forgotten his other case.'

'Does he ever forget?' There was a quizzical expression on Robert's face. 'Nearly six. Better clear up . . . Wednesday,' he reminded her. He spoke in short staccato sentences to hide the emotion that lay just beneath the surface.

Thea felt a wave of affection for him, resenting the fact that she could not love him and thus make life simple, the future secure. Julian was an enigma whose behaviour kept her in a state of nervous tension. She shrank from the idea that he was a philanderer, because it confounded all previous convictions.

'Wednesday,' she echoed. 'I shall look forward to it.'

He moved nearer to her, picked up her hand and kissed it before going quickly from the office.

She was wondering if she would see Julian again that evening, and if his last patient had gone, when he stepped out of the lift. She didn't speak, but crossed the large entrance hall to the front door. Julian hurried to open it for her. She looked up at him with a cold surprise.

'I'm glad I caught you,' he said quietly. 'My apologies

for my earlier behaviour. I don't usually express my anger in such a fashion.'

Thea gave him a withering look.

'No need to apologise. Nothing you did would surprise me,' she said icily as she struggled to suppress the desire his nearness awakened.

He stood there after she had gone, a little stunned, immobile. Robert spoke as he strode towards him.

'Are you coming in or going out?'

'Out,' Julian said briefly.

Robert knew that something had annoyed him and exclaimed as he reached his side, 'I'll be home in a matter of minutes and I'll take care of the calls as arranged.'

'I'll ring you when I get back. I shan't be late.'

'Fine. Time doesn't matter.'

Julian looked at him a trifle distractedly. 'Thanks.'

'By the way, will you do the same for me next Wednesday?' Robert asked.

'Certainly.' It was a crisp sound.

'I'm taking Thea to the theatre.' Robert couldn't keep the pleasure from his voice.

Julian merely nodded. They went out of the house together; nothing more was said. Julian recalled that Robert had previously mentioned the theatre to Thea in his presence . . . And as he drove to the Hardys' flat which was above the florist's shop in Western Road, he still smarted under Thea's scorn, unable to excuse his own incomprehensible behaviour. No one, he thought, had ever had the power to infuriate him as she, and he decided that, while he liked her, there was a deep-rooted antipathy that led to aggression, even dislike, on occasions. It did not make for a good relationship in a practice, he reasoned gloomily and, taking the issue further, he deplored the indiscretion of seeking Thea's help with Vicky. It was a false move stimulated by concern and circumstances, as was his confidence about the prospect of his ceasing to be Vicky's doctor when, as the situation grew more delicate, it would be almost an impossibility, although his instincts accepted the advisability of such a move.

It was in this mood of turmoil and depression that he faced the Hardys in what became a harrowing and shattering experience. Glynis Hardy had hysterics; her husband Philip seemed frozen in disbelief, while the horror of the facts seemed to bring about the disintegration of a family. There was no compassion; no prospect of forgiveness, although the father was at breaking point when he faced up to the consequences and inevitable death. Brenda sat immobile. She had seen, and told, Paul, leaving him to take in the tragedy and arranging to see him the following day. It was too vast a problem to absorb in an impassioned moment. In addition, they both wanted to talk to Julian at his rooms. That much had come out of the confession. They were both frozen into silence by the stark reality of the truth from which there was no escape and no hope. Now she divorced herself from her parents as she sat listening to a tirade she had known to be inevitable and which ended with her mother saying, 'You'll leave this house; we don't want it contaminated . . . I never want to see you again!'

Afterwards, driving to Vicky, Julian felt that he had been a witness in a old-fashioned melodrama where a pregnant daughter had been told, 'Never darken our doorstep again'. Now there was a curse dwarfing all other problems. How many more families would be facing the dilemma as the Hardys were doing, their ignorance and revulsion widening the abyss, shattering all hope of salvation? He felt drained of emotion as though he had fought some horrendous battle which only death could win. He was accustomed to drama, to terminal illness, but never before had he faced the fear and loathing of one human being for another, or encountered the dark hopelessness of being denied any signpost to point the way.

The juxtaposition of life in the Hardys' flat and what appeared to be the carefree atmosphere at The Drive house struck Julian incongruously as Briggs admitted him a short while later. He took a deep breath and changed his mood, knowing that Vicky would be upset were he to be depressed on the evening of her return.

Lionel came forward the moment Julian entered the hall, irritated by the fact that he was later than expected, and greeted him saying, 'Vicky's in bed; it's been a long day for her. I promised I'd send you up so that she can tell you all the details. I'll join you in a short while . . . you'll stay for a meal?'

The prospect of facing Lionel alone for a social hour or so was not, Julian thought with a gentle irony, 'what the doctor ordered', and he made some excuse covered by his profession and went up to the bedroom.

It was an off-white room, with light cherry furnishings. Massive windows looked out on the wide tree-lined drive and an air of elegance and femininity predominated. Vicky herself wore an off-white silk and lace negligee that swirled around her, emphasising her pale appealing beauty which, despite her physical condition, nevertheless hinted at the normal vivacity and enthusiasm in moments when life allowed her to enjoy it.

Her gaze seemed to melt into his as he said, 'I'm sorry I'm late. I've had a difficult case.'

'It's seemed an eternity since I got back this morning.' Vicky shrank a little further into the large down pillows. 'And heaven to be in this bed! They line them with bricks in hospital and I'm sure the sheets are made of sacking.' She added, 'But they were so *kind* to me, and I had every attention.' A little sigh escaped her.

'I want to check your blood pressure and pulse . . . satisfy myself. You realise you'll have to take things quietly?'

'They drummed it into me. No smoking or drinking!' She pulled a face. 'I shall miss the latter because I share that with you . . . Oh, Julian, it's so good to *see* you.'

'It's good that you're home.' His voice was restrained. 'Now.' He put the cuff of the sphygmomanometer around her arm as she pulled back her sleeve. A faint suggestion of expensive scent stole from her in a sensuous wave.

Her pulse was racing and Julian lowered his gaze as he busied himself with returning the sphygmomanometer to his medical case.

'You didn't expect my pulse to be normal, did you?' Her voice was low and her eyes as they met his were full of significance.

'Listen, Vicky——' he began anxiously.

She cut in. 'I *know*, and I'll be good, but——'

There came a faint knock at the door as, almost immediately. Lionel entered the room.

'Well?' he queried, and it registered subconsciously

that Julian was sitting on the bed and not in the chair beside it.

'Quite satisfactory. Rest, quiet and a bland diet.' He added, 'And a check-up in two weeks.'

'I want that to be arranged with Dr Sloane privately.'

Vicky fumed, telling herself that Lionel had spoilt everything by intruding at the wrong moment. There was so much she wanted to say to Julian, and an uncomfortable churned-up sensation started slightly in the ulcer area.

'Very well.' Julian didn't argue, feeling at a disadvantage. He was aware of the effect Lionel had on Vicky and the delicate situation generally.

'Will you be coming in tomorrow?' Lionel added, 'And shouldn't Vicky stay in bed for a few days?'

'Rest, yes; bed, not necessary. To get out on the patio and have some sea air. Take everything easily.'

'Well,' said Lionel in a clipped fashion, 'she's in the happy position of being able to follow that advice. Rose will take care of her. I can't get away, having had that—that abortive cruise. Waste of time and money . . . Responsible for all this.'

'That's behind us,' Vicky put in. She was beginning to feel hot and agitated.

Julian told them, 'No undue exertion for a while; take things gradually.' He tried to sound professional, but he was aware of Vicky's unease.

'*Will* you come in tomorrow?' She looked at him searchingly.

Lionel gave Julian an enquiring scrutiny.

'Yes,' he said swiftly. 'Now I must get back.'

Lionel said, after having gone with Julian to the front door and returned, 'A bit off, I thought. Comes late, and hasn't any time to spare. I'll never know that man.'

Vicky said fearfully, 'But you like Julian?'

'I didn't say I didn't like him. What's that got to do with it? I pay him; I can criticise him. He's spent enough time here recently——' There was a grudging irritation in the words.

Vicky cried, 'Oh, Lionel, don't start criticising Julian! I know you—once you begin to find fault with people, nothing's right about them.' Her voice rose. 'He's looked after me, seen me through so much——' She was getting upset, and Lionel sensed that it was the worst thing for her.

'Now then,' he began soothingly, 'there's no question of my doing anything to annoy Julian. My only concern is you. I'm going to have my own way from now on. It's been a bloody awful time. The house has been like a morgue without you, and I've been damned worried . . .' He subjected her to an intent questioning gaze. 'They talked of worry and stress in connection with all this?'

She fingered the lace on her negligee, avoiding his eyes as she said carelessly, 'Yes . . .'

'Well, darling——' The word sounded incongruous because, if he used an endearment, it was never 'darling'. 'It's just that,' he floundered, which, Vicky thought, was also unlike him, 'well, it's just that I think the answer to all this would be if we were to—to have another child as quickly as possible . . .'

Vicky cried out, a sensation of panic assailing her, her weakness making it impossible to have a verbal fight with him, 'I don't want to *think* about tomorrow, talk about it, or to have the past dragged up——'

Dismayed by her obvious panic, Lionel assured her hastily, 'All right, all right. I shouldn't have mentioned it, but I want to do everything for the best.'

Vicky felt guilty and mean, but she was incapable of standing up to an intimate discussion, and astonished that he should have initiated one at this moment.

'I'm sorry,' she muttered, putting her hand up to her forehead which was damp near the hairline, and her heart was thumping so that she could take her pulse by the banging sensation in her chest.

Lionel picked up her hand awkwardly.

'We'll talk some other time.' He knew he had been insensitive, and could not quite fathom his own mood. 'The last thing I want to do is to upset you.'

She murmured something inarticulate, then, 'Now you go and have something to eat,' she said with concern.

He looked down at her and at the bed they shared.

'I'll sleep in the spare room,' he said considerately, 'until you feel better. I don't want to disturb you.' He waited for what he hoped would be her rejection of the idea.

'Perhaps that would be better,' she agreed tentatively, 'I'm restless, too. If you don't mind, I'll settle down now——'

He nodded, a shadow of disappointment crossing his face. 'I'll send Rose up,' he promised, 'to do anything you——' He stopped as though a thought suddenly struck him. 'Would you like a nurse here?'

She insisted immediately, 'Good gracious, no! But thank you all the same. You're very good to me, Lionel.'

'I love you,' he said simply, and bent and kissed her cheek.

Sadly, and with relief, Vicky saw him go from the room.

During the next few days Thea behaved with a cool efficiency when in Julian's presence, supplying him with details of various cases and dealing with him through Miss Jenkins or Enid whenever possible. He could not have accused her of insolence. She was the practice nurse and no more, until she came upon him unexpectedly, head in hands and a stricken expression on his face.

Animosity vanished as she cried, 'What is it?'

He dropped his hands and squared his shoulders.

'Paul . . . positive. He and Brenda are coming to see me at eleven.'

A terrible silence fell. They looked at each other and Thea's belligerence dissolved, becoming so trivial as to be pathetic.

'They'd like you to be there.' He did not want to pull rank.

'I'll be there,' Thea promised softly.

Julian held her gaze and there was a strange appeal in it, like a man silently admitting that he was under strain generally; and, while she knew how deeply involved he was with the Hardy case, it didn't wholly account for his unease.

'It's been a hell of a time.' He made a sweeping gesture. 'And what can I do for these two tragic people? *Words*,' he added almost fiercely.

'Does he know?'

'Yes. He rang early. I'd only just spoken to the Southern—we've got a splendid liaison with the lab there, thank God. Whoever said, "It isn't what you know, but who you know", was a wise man.' He sighed, escaping for a second into normality.

Brenda Hardy and Paul Trent arrived promptly at eleven. They were both stricken and yet curiously composed. Paul was a tall athletic type who was a near genius with his hands, making much of the artistic products the Craft Centre sold—miniature toys, transport, furniture. Now he was pale, and as with Brenda, only his tragic eyes gave life to a parchment-shaded face. After the initial greetings, he said as they settled in their respective chairs, 'This isn't easy for any of us, Dr Fraser, and I know you can't give us a prognosis, but we can perhaps make it easier if we tell you what we've decided.'

Julian stood for a second before sitting down at his desk and resting his forearms upon it, hands clasped.

'Decided?' he echoed.

Thea drew in her breath.

'We're going to be married. Whatever lies ahead we shall face it together.'

It was the last thing Thea had considered.

'You see,' Brenda went on, 'we don't know how long we have, or what form the disease will take, but we can at least live a normal life until we're parted. We can face *death* together; but not life—apart.'

'I see,' Julian murmured, stunned.

Paul explained, 'I understood, and accepted, what happened in Brenda's life before she met me. I can't condemn it now because she's become a victim. Me too, ironically.' He paused before going on, his voice deepening, 'Oh, at first I thought I was going mad. I loathed everything and everybody. I hated Brenda and felt I was some unclean monster.' He looked at Julian and then at Thea. 'It took me two days before I realised I was thinking only of myself, not allowing for the agony Brenda must be suffering. Then I tried to picture life without her; the fact that no matter which way you viewed it, she was facing a death sentence.' He gazed at Brenda with a love that brought tears to Thea's eyes, and a lump to Julian's throat. The quiet dignity of the words, the depth of feeling, was like a benediction.

Brenda said quietly, 'You see, Dr Fraser; but do you *understand*?'

Thea's gaze met Julian's for a fraction of a second and she wondered how he would meet the situation were he and Vicky involved.

He said, his deep voice shaken, 'Oh, yes, I assure you I understand.'

Thea felt that a rough hand was squeezing her heart, robbing her of breath.

'We went over every phase of the situation, tried to allow for all eventualities, particularly if I should prove to be infected. This isn't an impulsive spur-of-the-moment decision: it's a commitment. If the test hadn't been positive, I should still have wanted Brenda to be my wife, no matter what type of life we were forced to lead. We already own a house, and it's furnished ready for when we were to be married . . . Now we shall be married as soon as it can be arranged. My parents have done nothing to dissuade us, although they are, of course, devastated. I told them before I came here that—' for the first time, he faltered and then hurried on, 'that the test was positive. I don't underestimate their horror or their suffering.'

'My parents,' Brenda said heavily, 'made me leave home the day after you spoke to them, Dr Fraser. I'm staying with Paul's family. The social side we can't deal with immediately. We shall have to tell our friends and allow for the prejudice and revulsion that's inevitable.'

Julian and Thea sat there, both realising that they were having a completely new experience in medicine; something they had never dealt with before and which, until definite symptoms manifested themselves, they were helpless even to diagnose.

Then came the question that made Thea tense, even fearful, as Paul said, 'Dr Fraser, will you continue to be our doctor?'

Julian didn't hesitate, his voice was strong and re-assuring. 'You're my patients and always will be. I'll do everything within my power to help you.'

They looked at each other with thankfulness and relief.

'We can never thank you for making this——Oh God, there are no words . . . we're still in a state of shock, but not a shock so great that we don't realise that being parted would be the greatest hell. For as long as we *can* we shall be together.' He added inscrutably, 'Who knows but that we may decide the length of time.'

Julian lifted his head and was about to comment, then thought better of it.

The room was very silent after they had gone. Their love for each other seemed to have left a power behind which neither Julian nor Thea would ever forget.

CHAPTER SIX

THE WEEKS passed and Vicky was pronounced fit. It had been a time of tension and suspense for Thea, whose relationship with Julian had been on a knife-edge. An uneasy calm seemed to have settled upon his association with Vicky, but there had been no mention of his ceasing to be her doctor. Yet every time her name was mentioned, Thea felt a strange foreboding, aware of how he abruptly changed the subject. On this occasion, however, he had no means of escape, because he had arranged to entertain Lionel, Vicky, Robert and herself at the restaurant attached to his flat, and Thea said directly, 'Is this a kind of "signing off" party for Vicky, now that she's well again?' The question was framed deliberately to have a *double entendre*. Her own emotions were so involved that she felt she must learn as much as possible about the situation, even if she incurred Julian's wrath in the process.

'It is,' he said stiffly, 'a gesture to return hospitality.' His gaze was critical.

She refused to be put off. 'You must forgive me, but you did once confide that you were going to cease to be Vicky's doctor.' The words rushed out, and she was amazed at her own daring.

Julian made no attempt to explain, but exclaimed tersely, 'Circumstances change. We'll hope that Vicky doesn't need my professional services from now on.' He looked awkward as he added, 'She's a very highly strung person.'

'Implying that——'

He cut in, 'Implying nothing; and this is a futile conversation. I hope you'll enjoy the evening and not analyse us all out of existence. I'm grateful for the support you've given Vicky these past weeks,' he added possessively, and might have been speaking as a husband.

Thea didn't want to feel the bitterness of jealousy, because Vicky didn't engender such emotion. She had an appeal, no matter what the circumstances, that touched the fringe of innocence, and seemed like a child pleading for a new toy. What was more, Thea knew she was unhappy and, contradictorily enough, suffered with her. Their mutual love for Julian was a secret bond, but one in which, from Thea's point of view, there was envy. It didn't matter how unworthy Julian might be, nothing could lessen the passionate love and desire she felt for him even in those moments when she told herself she hated and despised him. She wondered if she had been asked to dinner that night as an acknowledgment of his gratitude, or because she and Robert were classed together, even though their relationship had not radically changed.

Ellsmere Court, where Julian lived, was an elegant building, with a main hall richly furnished, from which smooth lifts bore the occupiers and visitors to the respective flats. It had the air of a hotel, with deep-piled carpets and glittering chandeliers. Thea went up to the third floor that evening with a sensation of trepidation. Robert had been delayed, or he would have escorted her. She thought as she rang the door bell and looked down the wide panelled corridor that it was both impressive and luxurious, but impersonal.

She waited a few seconds, surprised at the delay, then Julian answered her ring with a somewhat hurried, embarrassed greeting as he stood in the circular hallway, handsome in his cream jacket and black trousers. He met her gaze for an instant and swiftly stood aside for her to enter.

'I thought Robert would be with you,' he said as he shut the front door, adding in a breath, 'Vicky's here——'

'So,' Thea said deliberately, 'I see.' As she spoke she looked through to the large sitting room where Vicky sat in the depths of the sofa, surreptitiously returning her compact and lipstick to her handbag. She called out as Thea came towards her, 'You look terrific! That black-and-white dress is so smart.' Her voice was a trifle breathless. 'Lionel isn't here yet; I was early.'

The atmosphere was uneasy. Thea took in the familiar room with its peach carpet and hangings, which was en suite with the adjoining hall, spacious and attractively furnished. An expansive view of the sea brought the scene to life, and the now calm blue waters formed a striking mural.

It was then, as Julian came towards them, that Thea noticed the smudge of lipstick by his left jaw and ear; a smudge not immediately noticeable full-face. Her heart missed a beat, a sick jealousy mingled with fear lest Lionel should see it and not necessarily assume that it was she, Thea, who was responsible. There had never been more than purely formal greetings between Julian and Vicky in the presence of others, and their respective attitudes made jumping to conclusions inevitable.

Thea didn't hesitate as she said, 'You have a smudge by your left ear, Julian. I'm sure you won't mind my mentioning it before the others get here.' With that she gave him a direct meaning gaze and, half hesitating, and then awkwardly, he turned and went into an adjoining bedroom.

Vicky raised her eyes to Thea, who sat down beside her on the sofa. Colour mounted Vicky's cheeks. 'Thank goodness you noticed,' she whispered, her voice full of relief. 'It doesn't matter with you,' she added significantly, 'you know, anyway, don't you?'

Thea's pulse was racing. 'Yes, I know. But——'

Julian returned before any more could be said, making no comment as he exclaimed with *sangfroid*, 'I see no reason why we should wait for these latecomers, the champagne——'

Vicky cut in with forced gaiety, 'I'm going to have my first sip since I spoiled everything that night.' She was glad Thea had noticed the lipstick being fully aware of the dangers of the situation.

The door bell rang and Robert and Lionel stood there, having met in the lift.

'I doubt if my wife has arrived,' said Lionel in the tone of one who expected her always to be late—a habit which annoyed him.

'Thea and Vicky are both here,' Julian said discreetly, his manner smooth.

'Ah!' Lionel looked across the spacious hall and into the sitting room, his gaze going to Vicky and then to the champagne in the ice bucket. 'This is a very attractive apartment, Julian,' he added, 'you certainly know how to live a successful bachelor's life.'

Thea looked straight into Julian's eyes as the three

men entered the room, a cynical half-smile curving her lips.

Julian's jawline hardened, but he made no comment as he lifted the champagne bottle and opened it expertly.

Robert watched Thea, aware of her air of disapproval and at a loss to understand it. He had tried to fathom the relationship between Julian and Thea, without succeeding. It fluctuated between the formal and informal; between her being simply the practice nurse and then almost an intimate friend, when she talked more like a doctor whose knowledge far exceeded that with which she was credited; Julian accepting her at that level, recognising her diagnostic abilities and prepared to accept her judgments. That facet disturbed him most and emphasised what appeared to be an emotional closeness that confounded his assessments. As against that, he was disturbed by Julian's association with Lionel and Vicky, knowing full well that Lionel was not the attraction, and that Vicky was obviously emotionally involved—a dangerous complication. Several times that evening he found Lionel's gaze trained first on Julian and then on Vicky, a hard questioning expression in his eyes. It was not a relaxed evening. During dinner, they might have been playing a well-known piece of music in the wrong key. Conversation was staccato, with awkward silences when everyone began to speak at the same time. Once or twice Robert intercepted a meaning glance exchanged between Vicky and Thea while, for the most part, Vicky's eyes hardly left Julian's face.

It was while they were having coffee in the cream and gold restaurant that Lionel said conversationally, 'I've to go over to Rome in a fortnight's time . . . how about coming with me?' He eyed Vicky with deliberation.

'Rome!' She made it sound like the Antipodes. Her voice was breathless and apprehensive.

'What does your doctor have to say?' Lionel looked at Julian.

'That it's purely a matter of how Vicky feels.'

Lionel frowned. 'But she's fit again?'

'I'm perfectly fit,' Vicky assured him. 'But I can't say I'm very thrilled with these business trips. I hang around in hotel rooms while you're locked up with your business colleagues.' She paused and tried to sound natural. 'No, thank you . . . not this time.' She added with a little smile, 'When you're going to Venice on the Orient Express, I'll think about it!'

Thea noticed that Julian was looking deeply into his coffee cup, avoiding Vicky's swift gaze.

'Orient Express?' Lionel echoed the words in surprise. 'I didn't know you wanted to go——'

Vicky rushed in, 'Oh, Lionel, it was just a thought —half joking. At the moment I'm more than happy to be at home, enjoying being fit again . . . How long are you going for?'

'Four or five days,' he said easily. 'Monday to Friday.'

Vicky felt excited. She would manoeuvre something with Julian!

'I love Italy,' said Robert, noticing Julian's silence. 'I always feel happy there.'

Vicky changed the subject, her cheeks were flushed and she exclaimed brightly, 'I feel happy after my drink, but I wouldn't want any more . . . It's been a splendid evening, Julian.'

'I agree,' Lionel added.

'Pleasure,' murmured Julian, grateful that it was

coming to an end. He was aware of Thea's cold condemnation which was almost tangible, and had nothing with which to combat it. A little later he saw her leave the flat with Robert, and a curious depression settled upon him. Life was becoming too dangerous . . .

Lionel said later to Vicky, 'Why won't you come to Rome with me?'

They had returned from the evening with Julian, and were sitting out on the patio overlooking the rose garden. The light was fading and the sky was brushed with rainbows as the afterglow spread like magic, flooding the earth with a roseate glow.

'It isn't a question of not *wanting* to go with you,' she said carefully, 'just that I'm enjoying being well again and I don't, quite honestly, want the effort. You know I don't like flying . . . another time.'

He accepted that.

'I'll take you on the Orient Express,' he promised, somewhat irrelevantly.

She smiled at him, feeling she was pandering to a child to keep the peace. Her convalescence hadn't been an easy time, and his return to her bed traumatic, since she had put it off for as long as was tactful, not wanting any major upheaval.

'That would be lovely,' she said, the words meaning nothing, and the whole idea far away.

And suddenly, dramatically, like thunder crashing into deep silence, he asked, 'Is Julian in love with you?'

Vicky had a glass of mineral water in her hand and jerked the contents over her dress.

'*Julian*?' she managed to gasp. 'Whatever made you ask a question like that?'

Lionel was trying to keep calm.

'*Is* he?'

Vicky gave a little laugh.

'Oh, Lionel; do be sensible! Of course he isn't! He's my *doctor*! I've relied on him perhaps a little too much, but for goodness' sake don't get such ideas in your head. Julian is the last man, I should imagine, to go falling in love with his patients. You've said yourself that he isn't easy to know.'

'That's true, but there was just *some*thing in his manner tonight——'

'If you want to get near the truth, I think he and Thea had been involved in some quarrel. She was very offhand with him. Didn't you notice?'

'I was too busy watching *him*. He avoided looking at you . . . there was just *something*.'

'He and Thea behave very strangely,' Vicky persisted.

Lionel was working himself up, deaf to what was said.

'If I thought,' he thundered, 'that he ever made any—or that you felt anything for him——'

Vicky knew she must keep calm; a wrong move could be fatal.

'You're being insulting,' she said with quiet criticism. 'Obviously we've seen more of him recently; you can't be treated by a doctor without *seeing* him. *You've* invited him here,' she added deliberately, stressing the point, while knowing that she had manoeuvred most of the visits.

Lionel looked stubborn. He had that 'don't cross me' attitude which she feared.

'I'd ruin him . . . see that he was struck off. Make no mistake about that. He'd be finished—finished!' he shouted. 'No one takes advantage of my *wife*——' He paused and looked at Vicky with an unnerving gaze. 'Just you remember that, if you ever think you can make a fool of me.'

Vicky didn't risk getting into an argument, or over-protesting. She said calmly, 'Suppose you stop being utterly foolish and let's have an early night . . . it's getting cold——' She shivered deliberately.

Lionel was immediately concerned.

'Very well.' He got to his feet.

Vicky's heart slowed down a little. She put her arm through his and they walked indoors together. She felt as if she was on an ice-rink, rushing towards a disaster she could not avoid. There was a set determined expression on Lionel's face and she knew she had not convinced him so far as Julian's feelings were concerned, and when, later, she was sitting at her dressing table brushing her hair while he observed her from the bed, she said with confidence, 'You know, Lionel, you amaze me over Julian——' She spoke with a natural ease.

'Why?' It was a clipped, half-accusing exclamation.

'Because his relationship with Thea is so obvious! Why should he invite her tonight, for instance? Doctors don't automatically socialise with their practice nurses, and she's invariably been here with him.'

'At your invitation,' he growled.

Vicky brushed her thick hair and let it cascade from the brush in a sensuous movement which she knew attracted Lionel.

'You like her and are good friends,' he went on insistently. 'And there's Robert. He's obviously keen on her.'

'I agree.' Vicky half turned on the stool and gave Lionel a knowing look. 'But there's no question of Thea returning Robert's feelings. She and Julian are far too involved.'

Lionel seemed receptive. 'Has she told you that?'

'Not in so many words, but Julian has betrayed his feelings more than once.' Vicky had no compunction about the deception and was prepared to deploy any subterfuge to avoid suspicion.

'Well, there's one thing that will prove if you're right,' said Lionel with a stern finality.

She swivelled back to face the dressing table.

'And that?'

'*Time* . . . now come to bed.'

It was a day or two later during the lunch hour that Thea decided to replace some much-needed make-up at Hannington's, the large imposing store in North Street. It was a glorious day and she drove past the Grand Hotel and New Brighton Centre, glancing at the sea which lay like a sequined sari glittering in the sun, turned left into Market Street, and arrived at her destination. She was well known to the assistant in the department and was served quickly with friendliness and courtesy. The faint smell of exotic scent hung in the air and Thea looked around her with appreciation. She felt at home and wished she had the leisure really to shop instead of thinking she had an injection to give at two-fifteen. It was at that moment she noticed Julian and Vicky, in earnest conversation, a short distance away. She tried to avoid detection, but Vicky saw her and flashed a little intimate smile which, interpreted, suggested, 'I don't have to pretend to you.'

Julian's gaze met hers in a look of embarrassment, and he made a gesture as though he were about to leave.

It was too much, Thea thought angrily, to assume that

theirs was a chance meeting; yet why choose the foremost store in the town, where they would be most likely to run into their associates? She deliberately moved towards them.

'Quite a coincidence,' Julian said briefly.

Thea noticed that neither he nor Vicky had any purchases.

'I don't even remember what I want to buy,' Vicky smiled as she spoke.

But Thea felt irritated. Julian looked ill at ease.

'I must get back,' he said too quickly.

'So must I.' Thea didn't realise how cynical her expression was as her gaze met his.

Vicky spoke with sudden and unexpected longing. 'I wish we could go for a run in the country, or drive to the Devil's Dyke; it's so beautiful, and I love the Downs. Everybody is at work and has no time.'

They were both arrested by a certain poignancy in her attitude as she went on, 'I often think time is the most precious thing one human being can give to another.' There was a faraway look in her eyes as she seemed suddenly to come out of a trance and added, 'But I mustn't keep you.' There was something wistful in the observation that matched the sadness in her dark eyes. She was a rather pathetic, lonely figure at that moment.

Thea felt a pang; misery settled darkly upon her.

Julian hurried away. Vicky, with a wintry smile at Thea, said quietly, 'I'll do my shopping,' and disappeared.

Thea rang Julian on his private line later that afternoon.

'Could you spare me ten minutes at my flat this evening? I've something I want to say to you, and it's impossible to guarantee any peace here.' She added swiftly, 'Any time.'

He didn't hesitate, although he was surprised.

'Seven-fifteen?'

'Very well . . . Trevor's coming at half-past.'

'I've missed him lately; he doesn't seem to have been around.' Julian was sincere.

'He's working on an exhibition for the Hayward,' Thea told him.

'Oh! . . . Seven-fifteen,' Julian repeated.

The line went dead.

Julian was punctual. It was a warm July evening and he settled in an armchair, whisky in hand, looking both puzzled and apprehensive. Then he said, 'I hope this mysterious summons has nothing to do with Trevor's health—or anyone else closely associated with you.'

Thea, in a loose, kimono-type pale jade dress, felt suddenly nervous and full of fear. All her resolution and whipped-up anger vanished as she looked at him, his power robbing her of strength, as she said, 'Nothing like that.'

He gazed down into his glass and then raised his eyes to meet hers unnervingly. 'What, then?'

She knew that prevarication would serve no good purpose and she said quietly, but with conviction, 'Your relationship with Vicky.'

The sudden silence was heavy and unnerving, as he repeated her question with a sense of outrage.

'And *what* has my relationship with Vicky to do with you?'

Thea breathed deeply, fighting to overcome the dryness of her mouth and the thudding of her heart.

'Nothing; but my concern for the practice and your

professional reputation has everything to do with me.'

Julian challenged, 'I dispute that. The practice and my reputation are *my* concern. Will you kindly keep out of my affairs? Of all the impertinence! To invite me *here*——' He stopped, speechless.

Thea was trembling. She had not thought it would be easy, but her love for him had given her false courage, a strength of purpose that was now dwindling.

Again there was a heavy silence, which she broke by saying, 'I could hardly go into this at Adelaide Crescent and I've no desire to interfere, but Vicky is your *patient*! For God's sake! You could be struck off.' She shook her head. 'I'm genuinely fond of Vicky, but she's dangerous —a married woman.' She spread her hands in a gesture of desperation. 'You have everything to lose. Can't you *see*?'

He went white with anger, his eyes narrowing, his lips a thin line of suppressed fury.

'Oh, I *see*.' His voice held a deadly calm. 'You've made your own judgments——'

'On observation, not suspicion,' countered Thea, staring him out.

'None of this is your concern,' he emphasised, 'but the mere fact of your interference makes me realise that I've allowed you too much latitude. Not only do you want to run the practice, but my private life as well.'

Their eyes met accusingly.

'That's unfair,' she protested, 'and you know it.' She went on, 'Your reputation is at stake and, recently, it would have been easy to believe that you and I had achieved a degree of—of friendship.' Faint colour rose in her cheeks. 'Obviously I've misjudged your attitude, but irrespective of what you may think of me and my shortcomings, my fears remain. Lionel is suspicious; the way he studied you the other night——'

As she spoke, the incident of the lipstick was uppermost and led to an awkward silence.

'I suggest,' Julian said tartly, 'that we end this conversation. I shall pretend it never happened. From now on we're professional colleagues; you're a good member of our team and I shouldn't want to lose you, but any further interference in my affairs, or reference to Vicky Holford, and our association ends.'

Thea wanted to cry out that it had already done so, but she could not face up to the torment of parting; of walking out of his life and leaving him in the danger that lurked to destroy his career. Vicky was, she realised, appealing, and she would probably see the wreckage of his professional life as a small price to pay for their being together. There was no question about her unhappiness, or that it had brushed off on Julian. And now that he had heard the truth from Thea's lips, a dark shadow seemed to have fallen upon his face.

The silence between them was tense and he broke it by saying, 'Trevor will be here in a minute. I have great admiration for your father,' he added, as though he must restore some normality.

'So have I,' she said softly, 'and that's very important. One can love a person without liking them—at any level. The *liking* is the stability. I don't see enough of him, but he understands . . . and here he is.'

'Thea?'

She was always aware of his using her name because, in the beginning, he had done so spasmodically; therefore it had a significance, as did her calling him Julian.

'Yes?' He got to his feet and she to hers as she went to greet her father.

'I know,' he said, his mood swinging to justice, 'you have my interests at heart. And probably you and Robert discuss the issue, but when it comes to it——'

'You will, as we all do, go to destruction in your own way.' Thea's voice was hard. 'You've left me in no doubt of your feelings.' She spoke as she went to the door, Julian following to leave.

Trevor stood there, unsteadily, looking ill. Thea called his name, alarmed.

He managed to say, 'Pain in . . . my chest.'

They got him to the sofa, and Julian's fingers went to his pulse.

'Where's the pain?' Julian asked.

Trevor indicated the upper part of his chest.

'Across there and . . . left arm.'

Thea poured out a small whisky and water. Julian nodded approvingly and held the glass to Trevor's lips. At this stage alcohol was a help.

Trevor bore the tight, heavy constricting pain with fortitude. It had not been throbbing or knife-like, and he had consoled himself for that reason, without realising he had all the symptoms of *angina pectoris*.

Thea crouched beside the sofa, looking beseechingly at Julian for reassurance, their immediate differences forgotten in the crisis. Her thoughts raced: the complications of angina being that a clot might form in the coronary artery and cause a coronary thrombosis.

'Ah,' Trevor murmured after a few minutes, 'that's better . . . sorry to startle you.' The pain had gone, but he felt weak and shaken. 'I've been working too hard,' he admitted, speaking slowly. 'Couldn't get it right.'

Thea reflected anew how she wished he would marry again, for while his creature comforts were taken care of by Mrs Kingsley, his elderly housekeeper, the companionship and love were missing. Even now, he looked an attractive fifty-two-year-old, his grey hair giving him a distinguished air.

'We'll check you out tomorrow,' Julian said firmly, 'and do an ECG . . . Oh, yes,' he insisted, as Trevor protested that he was perfectly all right and didn't want any fuss; that he'd had the pain once before, but that it had gone away without any trouble. 'Meanwhile,' Julian went on authoritatively, 'you'll rest. And I mean rest; no exertion.'

'And you'll stay tonight,' Thea insisted. 'You have an overnight bag here.'

Trevor agreed. 'No problem with the car! I walked. A bit far, perhaps.' He gave Julian a faint smile. 'You medical gentlemen are always telling us to walk to avoid heart attacks!' He added dubiously, 'If I've had one.' He made a gesture and got up to go to the bathroom, and while his gait was a little unsteady, he declined Julian's support.

Thea watched him disappear, and suddenly a wave of fear and misery overwhelmed her, unnerving her so that she covered her face with her hands and gave a little sob.

The next thing she knew was that Julian's arms were protectively around her shoulders.

CHAPTER SEVEN

EVEN IN that moment of stress and anxiety, Thea was electrified by Julian's body against hers, as he said in a low comforting voice, 'I'm satisfied he'll be all right.'

She looked up at him, weakened by her chaotic emotions, and immediately drew away, not daring to relax. Her attitude swirled them back to formality.

He said stiffly, 'I'll stay to help him into bed.' His gaze held hers masterfully. 'Don't let him see you upset. *Emotion* is the worst possible thing for him!' The word was uttered as though it offended him. A dangerous tension crept into the atmosphere, evidence of their earlier stormy dissension. Thea returned to the sofa immediately she heard her father's footsteps. He sat down and leaned back against the cushions, saying, 'I've spoilt the evening.'

Thea corrected swiftly, 'Julian was just leaving when you arrived. We'd only had practice matters to discuss.' She didn't realise how frosty the words sounded. 'Now,' she went on gently, 'bed for you.' She got to her feet. 'I'll put everything ready.'

Trevor didn't protest; while the pain had gone, he was very tired.

A little later Julian saw him into bed.

'A sedative,' he suggested, thinking he could get the prescription from an all-night chemist. He felt Trevor's pulse again, relieved that it was steady, if a little rapid.

'No, thank you,' Trevor protested. 'I sleep like a log

and I never take tablets! This is nothing,' he insisted. 'I've just been pushing myself too hard . . . must slow down.'

Julian weighed up the situation and let him have his way.

'Now,' he said as he was about to leave, 'you've only to ring if you need me——'

'Thanks, Julian. Very grateful you were here.'

Thea saw Julian to the door.

'I've told Trevor,' Julian repeated, '"You've only to ring, no matter what time", but I'm satisfied that he'll have a good night. We'll do an ECG tomorrow and I'll ring Hugh Mason. I believe in a second opinion.'

'Thank you . . . sorry I let go.'

He made a gesture to convey that it was natural and added, 'Very often it isn't until a person is ill that we realise how much he or she means to us.'

She flashed him a significant look.

'True; you have reason to know . . . Goodnight.'

A dark anger spread over his features. He left without another word.

As she shut the door, a wave of depression dragged her down into a dark pit, but she squared her shoulders and took a deep breath.

Trevor opened his eyes, smiling at her as she went into the bedroom—a bright room with Laura Ashley furnishings in pale green and lilac. As she sat down on the matching frilled duvet she slipped her hand in his and said, 'When I suggested we keep an overnight bag in our respective flats, I had drink-driving in mind, not your——'

He cut in, 'I'm fine. It's good to be here.'

A lump came into her throat. Julian's words echoed,

and she knew how true they were. She *had* never realised just what her father meant to her until now. Disobeying her professional rules, she persisted, 'And you're *sure* you're all right?'

A sleepy expression spread over his face.

'You're . . . fussing . . . nurse,' he murmured, and relaxed into a restful sleep.

Thea sat there, tears rolling down her cheeks as she noiselessly got to her feet, kissed him on the forehead and went slowly from the room, leaving the door open.

Julian telephoned her early the following morning and having heard that Trevor slept well, seeming none the worse for his attack, said, 'Bring him along as early as he can comfortably make it. I want Robert to go over him thoroughly and as we've access to an ECG machine with Dr Wingate here, that's no problem. Hugh Mason is in London this week, but we can see how things go, and make another appointment if necessary.'

And Thea was thinking, 'Why Robert to examine Trevor?' She said unguardedly, 'I thought you would look after my father?'

'I'm the gynaecological part of the set-up, Robert is the general expert and is particularly good where cardiology is concerned. I've stressed this before.'

'In very different circumstances.' The words slipped out.

There was a cold withdrawn note in his voice as he said, 'Bring your father along as soon as he feels like it.' The conversation ended.

Robert was sorry that Trevor had need of medical advice, but grateful that he had been given the task of looking after him. He had a word with Thea, who was about to start surgery. 'I've arranged with Dr Wingate for an ECG in half an hour.'

'How different it all is when the patient is a relative,' said Thea, meeting Robert's gaze with silent appeal.

Robert reassured her. 'You know everything will be done. He's your *father*, Thea, and means a great deal to me.' The words emphasised the bond between them, and even in that anxious moment Thea realised how much Robert, in turn, meant to her, and what a waste her love for Julian really was.

Trevor had a thorough examination, finally, at the rooms of Dr Wingate, lying on the couch to have the ECG with electrodes placed on the chest wall and limbs. Trevor was intrigued to watch the moving paper-strip recording the results.

Back in his own consulting room, Robert looked at Trevor half-questioningly.

'I want the truth,' Trevor said without hesitation. 'I know it's my heart, and if you want me to have another attack,' he added wryly, 'just be evasive!'

'Very well.' Robert spoke understandingly. 'You have angina.'

'The complaint is familiar to me, naturally,' Trevor admitted, 'in these days. But what exactly *is* it?'

'A narrowing of the coronary arteries. The blood supply to the heart muscles is reduced. But in your case, with treatment and commonsense living, you should be able to go on more or less normally. Glyceryl trinitrate will both stave off an attack and take away the pain when it starts. No smoking, climbing, walking against the wind, heavy meals.' Robert paused, then, 'The tablets will be your friend, and if you know you've got to exert yourself, take one as a precaution. Don't be afraid to do so; there's no virtue in it. Oh, yes; avoid emotion, excitement, argument—and don't overwork.' He stressed the last warning.

'At least I can have a drink,' Trevor said humorously, 'because Thea gave me a whisky with Julian's permission.'

Robert nodded. 'An alcoholic drink can be a useful alternative to a sedative in an emergency.'

'Then I must have a daily emergency,' came the dry reply. 'Moderation?'

'Exactly.'

'Thank God for small mercies!'

Robert had to laugh. He wished all his patients were of Trevor's calibre. But a serious note crept into his voice as he said, 'Now, stress and worry—have you any particular worries?'

Trevor didn't mince matters.

'I worry about Thea,' he admitted.

Robert wasn't surprised. 'So do I . . . I want to marry her.'

'If that happened I shouldn't have any more worries,' Trevor told him honestly.

'Thank you—I appreciate that. It won't be for want of trying . . . it *isn't*,' Robert corrected, 'that I haven't already tried. One doesn't want to become a bore.'

'You would never be that to her. I don't think she realises her true feelings for you,' Trevor said frankly.

'Meaning I should take her by storm?' Robert gave a little laugh.

'If you like . . .'

'I'll bear that in mind . . . now,' Robert temporized, 'to get back to you; you're healthy in every other way. You could outlive us all. There's no prognosis other than with the treatment and reasonable care, you should go on for years. If you feel pain coming on and you're walking, stop. Have your tablets handy, and I insist that, just now, you rest. No work; be a cabbage. Don't go out if there's a gale! I know you aren't the type to make yourself an invalid, but don't overdo it.'

'I won't.' Trevor thought of the painting that was unfinished, inspiration seeming to elude him, the tension agonising. 'But I must work. The stress will be far greater *not* doing so.'

'Give yourself a day or two,' Robert said firmly. He wrote out a prescription for trinitrate, then opened a drawer in his desk, handing Trevor a tablet from it.

'Take this now,' he said, pouring out some water from a thermos jug into a glass. 'It will make your head spin, but it'll soon go off . . . I'll get Thea to run you home.'

'Decrepit old fellow!' Trevor gave a weak chuckle. 'Thea's got her job to do. A taxi——'

'You just sit there quietly,' Robert ordered, as he left him and went into Thea's office where a patient was on her way out.

Thea's eyes and expression matched the fear in her question, 'How is he?'

Robert put her in the picture without any deception.

She listened and then cried, 'It's the uncertainty!'

'Never allow him to sense your fear,' Robert warned. 'You know as well as I that with treatment there's every chance of a good life span. Uncertainty walks with us all. He has the right temperament and will never live at half-mast, while obeying the rules. The patient can do so much. Some of them are scared of their own shadow. Not Trevor!' He smiled endearingly.

Thea's eyes glistened. 'Thank you,' she said softly. 'Do you mean that?'

She stared at him in surprise. 'Of course. What a thing to ask!'

'Then come and have a drink with me tomorrow evening. You've avoided me lately.'

She knew it was true. She couldn't face decisions.

'Very well—I'd like to.'

As she spoke she saw Julian standing in the doorway, his having hurried from his departing patient and anxious for news, fearing confirmation of his own diagnosis. When he heard the verdict he just looked at Thea with deep understanding, saying, 'I know Robert will have reminded you that with proper medical care, there's no reason why he may not live a relatively normal life for many years. It won't hurt to endorse his opinion.'

She nodded. 'It's so easy to think of one's parents as immortal.'

Julian and Robert exchanged glances. Their respective parents were perfectly fit at that moment.

Robert noticed that Thea didn't take her gaze from Julian's face and said swiftly, 'Thea's going to run Trevor home.'

'Of course,' Julian agreed. 'How are your appointments—as opposed to vetting our patients first?'

'Far too heavy to allow me more than the lunch hour,' she replied.

'Indispensable!' Robert exclaimed.

Julian made no comment, but at that moment Enid appeared in the open doorway, saying hurriedly, 'Mrs Holford is here, Dr Fraser, and wants to know if you can spare her just a few minutes.' She added, 'Your next patient has just arrived.'

'And who is that?' Julian's voice was clipped.

'Mrs Beckett.'

He seemed relieved.

'She's usually early and won't mind . . . yes, I'll see Mrs Holford.'

He didn't look at either Robert or Thea as he went quickly from the room.

Robert met Thea's gaze in an exchange of concern.

'I'm beginning to be worried about the Holford business,' he said gravely, and then, realising that this was not the time to discuss the matter, said, 'Now come and collect Trevor.'

Julian went into his consulting room and Vicky arrived almost immediately afterwards. He got up from his desk and greeted her from his position behind it, indicating the patient's chair.

'I've asked you not to come here,' he warned, and there was a note in his voice that made her heart hurt. 'I have a patient waiting and I make a point of not running late.'

She looked pathetic and vulnerable.

'Don't be cross,' she begged. 'But you didn't ring yesterday and——'

He explained about Trevor, and she was genuinely dismayed. There was something about her that made it impossible to upset her. Her persistence had a naïvety which added to the dangers of the situation. All that Thea had said to him re-echoed and he exclaimed a little desperately, 'Vicky, you must *see*——'

'I do: I love you. It's a kind of agony that makes me feel ill,' she whispered appealingly. 'And I wanted you to know that Lionel is going to Rome this Friday until Wednesday.' Her eyes met his in a significant look. 'I thought if you knew, we could arrange something.'

Julian looked, and felt, agitated. She sat there—a dangerous menace—and he exclaimed, 'Vicky——' and stopped. The minutes were ticking away and all he seemed aware of was Thea's words, 'She's your *patient*——'

'I'll see you, but you must go now. We must *talk*.' He stood up and then walked towards the door, avoiding physical contact as he opened it.

'Oh, *yes*,' Vicky agreed thankfully, looking at him with an adoring gaze. 'I could come to you——'

'I'll telephone.'

'Saturday,' she whispered, one foot in the corridor on her way out. There was an appealing expression in her voice. 'Early.'

'Yes.'

Satisfied, she brightened and walked away, leaving behind a faint fragrance of expensive scent.

Julian hurried back to his desk and flicked down the intercom.

'Send Mrs Beckett in,' he said, trying to sound normal, the feeling of guilt subsiding as he realised he had only kept her waiting five minutes. The memory of Vicky lingered disturbingly.

Robert didn't ask Thea where she wanted to go for a drink the following evening, and she made no comment when he took the Ditchling road out of Brighton, past Hollingbury Park on the right. Ditchling itself was a quaint village lying in the shadow of one of the highest peaks of the South Downs, its main street winding down the hill, timbered cottages and an old gabled house by the church gate, completing a picture painted by history. Anne of Cleves, Queen of England for a few months, had once lived in the half-timbered house with its Tudor chimneys, outside stairway and clustering roofs. Up on the Beacon was a dewpond which, to everyone, is an intriguing mystery; and even for those motoring past, there is a view of Clayton's Jack and Jill windmills across the common, to say nothing of Ditchling Gibbet, railed round with a cockerel on the top, testimony to the day in 1734 when they hanged a pedlar for murdering three people at an inn.

Thea realised that the summer had seemed bound up with Vicky, and she had missed the usual drives out that had previously been part of her life. Her love for Julian, also, had absorbed her to the exclusion of everything else.

'I've become thoroughly dull,' she said suddenly. 'It's good to be here like this.'

'I know an old inn nearby. They serve snacks.' He added forcefully, 'I'm not in the mood for a heavy meal.'

Thea shot him a sideways look of surprise. He sounded almost aggressive.

'Nor I,' she retorted. 'The shock of Trevor . . . somehow I feel I should be with him——'

'No,' came the emphatic comment. 'I've seen him today and so have you—he said so. Go along normally.'

'Marie Young heard that he wasn't well,' Thea went on. 'Vicky told her. She's going to see him about six.'

'An elusive woman,' Robert remarked. 'So often she was supposed to be coming to the Holford house, but I never met her. It would be a good thing if your father had a close friend—female.'

'I'd like the right stepmother,' Thea announced with finality. 'Marie Young is a widow in the same age group.'

They lapsed into silence until Robert drew up at the

Downs Inn, a Regency building with low bowed windows and an atmosphere that escaped ye olde worlde. It was candlelit, with only a murmur of voices and no intrusive music of any kind. They chose a seat away from the bar—a monk's bench with royal blue cushions and a circular polished table. Flowers filled the wide stone fireplace.

'Far from the madding crowd,' Robert remarked when they had been served their respective drinks—Robert a whisky, Thea a dry sherry.

Thea felt the mounting tension and knew this was not going to be a leisurely, uneventful evening.

Robert said, without preamble, 'Months ago, you told me that you'd come to me no matter what the trouble. I don't think you've kept that promise.'

Thea's heart seemed to miss a beat; a wave of apprehension made her shiver.

'That rather depends on what you mean by "trouble",' she suggested evasively.

'You could begin with the Julian and Vicky situation,' he said bluntly, his gaze meeting hers in direct challenge. 'Did you hope that silence would make it go away? Or that I was blind? You've been very friendly with Vicky and I've an idea that she's confided in you.'

Thea felt annoyed. 'If she has, then that demands loyalty on my part,' she said coldly.

'And loyalty to Julian,' he suggested almost accusingly.

'What else would you expect? The practice comes into it, and you're part of that,' she reminded him.

'Ah,' he said significantly, 'so you appreciate the wider issue.'

Thea did not want to discuss Julian in case, inadvertently, she betrayed her feelings.

'Like you, I'm not blind either,' she snapped. 'And I don't see the point of our coming out for a drink if this is the type of conversation we're to have!'

He protested, 'If we're the friends you . . . oh, hell, Thea! I'm tired of this nonsense. *Friends!* I no more want to be your friend than I need a hole in the head! It's farcical. Since we went to the theatre you've brought down a blind, while I've watched you swing from one mood to the other in your dealings with Julian. That's one reason why I've brought the subject of Vicky up now.' He shot the question at her. '*Have* you an influence over him?'

'None,' she said emphatically. 'As you've been witness to—I'm an employee and nothing else.' There was bitterness in her voice, but she added more gently, 'He was good to Trevor——'

'He hasn't been the same man since Vicky was taken ill that night. Incidentally, I ran into Lionel. Did you know he's going away this Friday—that the Rome trip has been put forward?'

Thea looked surprised.

'No.' The thought streaked through her mind that the fact might have had something to do with Vicky's visit to the rooms the previous day.

'He seemed very full of himself, I must say . . . Thea?' His expression and voice changed.

'Yes?' What was the question going to be? She felt anxious, her emotions chaotic, her feelings indecisive.

'I can't go on like this.' He added sharply, 'In fact I've no intention of doing so. Either you agree to marry me, or we become merely two people working in the same profession.'

Thea drew in her breath sharply. It was the last

ultimatum she had ever imagined.

'But you——'

'I've avoided rushing you,' Robert said, 'and I've brought you here tonight so that we could talk without any sexuality to confuse you.' He looked at her directly. 'You weren't indifferent to my kiss that evening at your flat when I first asked you to marry me.'

Thea knew that to be true. Robert was not the tame friend, but he was one whom she had set aside in her absorption with Julian.

She did not pretend. 'You're a very attractive man.'

'Thank you, but I don't merely want to *attract* you. You spoke of wanting marriage to be for life. So do I.' A faint smile touched his lips. 'So I'm offering you a life sentence, and I want a verdict now.' His words came forcefully and he held her gaze in a long inescapable look of determination.

It was a moment when her decision hung in the balance. The peace, security and emotional safety were a temptation she could hardly resist. All the aching longing that went with her love for Julian, the torment of dissension, would be over once she became Robert's wife; she would have a goal to work for, a new life to build, instead of wasting it on a man in love with a married woman who was his patient. Those were the facts, and she could not ignore them.

She said a little breathlessly, 'Just give me the weekend . . . I'll tell you on Monday.' Her voice was gently appealing. 'I don't want to allow the emotion of this moment to influence me, or pretend more than I feel.'

'You said those words to me last time.' There was a note of gloom in his voice.

'This isn't "last time",' she corrected him. 'A great deal has happened since then, and I'd like to think I'm the wiser.'

'Very well,' he agreed, 'Monday.'

Thea was trembling and on the brink of giving way, the hopelessness of her position so far as Julian was concerned turning a knife in her heart.

They left the inn a little later. It glowed in the blue darkness. Venus shone against a new moon, and the light over the downs seemed a benediction.

The telephone was ringing when Thea let herself into the flat. She hurried to it and heard Julian's voice.

'I've just come in.' She added deliberately, 'I've been over to Ditchling with Robert.'

He made no comment on that, but asked, 'Could I see you on Sunday?' His voice was urgent as he added, 'There's a matter I want to discuss.'

'I'm having lunch with Trevor, but the evening——'

'Very well—the evening. About six?'

She agreed.

His voice, low and unsettling, weakened her as he said quietly, 'Goodnight, Thea.'

Slowly she replaced the receiver.

What matter could Julian possibly want to discuss? Her leaving the practice? A spark of annoyance flared. It would be ideal if she could tell him that she was going to marry Robert. A cynical expression touched her lips. What difference would that make to him? Robert's words about Lionel going to Rome on Friday re-echoed, her thoughts disjointed, her emotions taut, while her imagination ran riot as she contemplated Julian and Vicky freed from Lionel's surveillance.

Vicky rang Thea that Friday evening. She sounded

bright and excited, and wanted Thea to come to see her and have a drink, adding that Lionel had gone to Rome. 'I must talk to you,' she said, her voice a trifle subdued. 'There's so *much*, Thea, and——' She paused. 'Do come?'

'Tomorrow evening,' Thea suggested deliberately.

Immediately Vicky said frankly, 'I'm going to see Julian . . . sorry, but I know you understand. The opportunities . . .' Her voice trailed away.

Thea didn't pretend to be sympathetic; instead, she suggested, 'We'll leave it over.'

'You sound annoyed . . . oh, Thea, don't be cross! I *do* want to talk to you.'

'We'll arrange it,' she promised.

'But while Lionel is away.' It was an urgent sound. 'He seems to resent my going out or seeing people these days.'

'When is he coming back?'

'On Wednesday.' She added with slight confusion, 'Could we make it lunch on Monday?'

Thea sensed that Tuesday evening would be spent with Julian.

'I'll try.' There was a tentative note in the agreement.

'Oh, good. A lot can happen in a weekend . . . I'll get Rose to make us something simple, but special.'

As Thea put the receiver down, a presentiment struck her. Lionel's absence seemed an ill omen, destined to precipitate a crisis.

Julian made no reference to his telephone call when he saw Thea the following morning. She was conscious of his smart appearance and of his somewhat grave demeanour as he said, 'Mrs Bell is coming in for a smear this morning and I want you to check the usual things, paying particular attention to her blood pressure. Take it both sitting and lying down. Miss a trick with her and her husband will have me in the stocks!' A smile broke out unexpectedly on his face, then grew to curiosity as he noticed the roses in a vase on the filing cabinet. He looked at her, expecting a comment, but Thea remained silent. They were from Robert, and she enjoyed Julian's obvious interest, which he immediately endeavoured to conceal by glancing swiftly away. 'Oh,' he went on, 'you'll notice an appointment for Mr and Mrs Trent——'

'Brenda Hardy previously,' she said in a breath.

'Yes.' He eyed her with serious contemplation. 'Would you prefer that I do all the checking——'

Thea didn't hesitate. 'I'll do the routine things as usual,' she said, holding his gaze.

'Thank you, Thea.'

She wondered why her name sounded almost an endearment, even when uttered normally.

'And I'd like *you* to bring them up.' Julian's gaze fell on the calendar that stood on her desk. 'Friday,' he said, with what she felt to be significance. 'But not the thirteenth.'

'Friday being a special day!' she exclaimed.

Immediately he tensed. 'I don't follow.'

'The end of the working week and, even for doctors, the promise of a respite sometimes!'

'Ah.' Julian spoke on a note of relief.

Thea felt he was a man walking on eggshells, alert to every challenge.

There was something exceptionally brave and yet poignant about Brenda and Paul Trent as they walked into Thea's office. They came in with a quiet dignity and an aura of happiness. Thea checked their respective blood pressure, temperature, respiration, and then said, 'Now come along to see Dr Fraser.' She smiled at Brenda in answer to her unspoken question. 'Yes, I'll take you up.'

Thea thought that Julian had never been more charming and understanding as he said, after the usual greetings, 'Now let's see, how long have you been married?'

'Three months. If anything should happen to us tomorrow,' said Paul with a manly pride, 'those months would have atoned for everything. You were so supportive, Dr Fraser, and you, Nurse. It was a spur that gave us confidence.' He looked at Brenda and the love that united them was like an aura. But inside, Thea wept because they were walking towards their doom. Yet couldn't that be said of everyone? Life gave only one guarantee—that of death, and she was not morbid in the observation. She was in a profession that emphasised this more than any other and, she told herself, to waste *today* was wishing life away. Only the *moment* was important. Her own problems, uncertainties and torments withered.

Julian managed to invite their confidence. Brenda's parents were still irreconcilable; his full of understanding. They had discovered their true friends and Brenda was working with one who supplied and arranged flowers to, and for, the hotels. Paul was still with the Craft Centre and had confided in the owner.

It was Brenda who voiced the haunting fear, and appealed for hope.

'Do you think there'll be a cure found soon, Dr Fraser?'

'The research is world-wide,' he replied. 'The time factor?' He sighed. 'No one can hazard any guess.' He smiled at Brenda. 'Now let's have a look at you.'

Thea took Brenda into the examining room. She looked radiant with the happiness that love brings, and made the words 'A woman is beautiful when she loves and is loved' so very true. 'You've been so good to me,' she said almost humbly. 'I don't feel a leper, as my parents made me feel. That hurt won't go away, neither will it spoil what Paul and I have.' There was a little wistful note in her voice as she added, 'We can never have children, but I'd like to think that, had it been possible, I would never have rejected them, no matter what they'd done.'

Thea looked at her as she got on to the examining couch, slim, firm-limbed, with small rounded breasts, and groaned inwardly. She could not bear to think that there was no resistance against disease in that seemingly perfect body and that any infection could mean death. Also that sexual contact . . . She dragged her thoughts back to her job. Reflections were not in order. A little shiver went over her as she felt the enormity and devastation of the disease, together with the thankfulness that she herself had never been promiscuous. It brought to mind Howard Flemming and how long it was since she had seen him. It would have been very easy to have had a relationship with him, irrespective of the fact that he wanted to marry her. Colour rose in her cheeks. Robert too, given the right circumstances, an extra drink . . . There, she thought, but for the grace of God, could have gone I. The fact that Howard and Robert were medically safe did not eradicate the dangers of a stolen hour . . .

The examinations were satisfactory. Julian suggested another appointment in six months, more to give a sense of security than a belief that such a precaution could in any measure stay the course of events.

'And should we not be . . .' Paul's voice shook slightly.

'Any trouble of any kind, just get in touch with me,' Julian reassured them.

They looked at each other with confidence, each knowing that the slightest ailment meant the possibility of death, and each determined to live as normally as possible, loved and loving, two people conveying an impression of health and happiness while living in the shadow of tragedy.

Thea thought of Robert as she saw them go. They represented all that was best in marriage, and its security struck her with a sudden urgent desire to escape from her present vacillation.

Robert saw her for a few seconds between patients.

'This is going to be the longest weekend of my life,' he said gloomily. 'What has Monday got that today hasn't?'

'Time in which to make adjustments and think things through.' Thea paused, remembering Julian's visit on Sunday, reluctant to mention it—afterwards, to her regret. She felt the influence of his appealing expression, a little afraid of its persuasive effect. She managed to hasten away as Enid reminded her of her next patient.

Saturday filled Thea with a sense of foreboding. She could not get Julian and Vicky out of her mind, and she felt she was waiting for a storm to break as she went for a swim, did some shopping and called on a patient-cum-friend who had a quaint Regency house near the Lanes, deciding, when the visit was over, to return to her flat and have a quiet evening. It was as she drove past the Palace Pier that to her astonishment and dismay she saw Lionel in a hire car.

CHAPTER EIGHT

FOR A SECOND Thea thought she must be mistaken and then, with a little shudder making her icy, she knew this was not so. Swiftly, desperately, she swung her car around and raced to Julian's flat, praying that no police car was in sight as she broke the speed limit. She didn't know exactly what she would do when she arrived, but she felt certain Vicky would be there and it seemed vital that she reached them. Lionel was not in Brighton for nothing; neither had he lied about the trip to Rome without having a good reason. The word 'good' she felt sure was a misnomer.

She stood, heart thumping, at the door of Julian's flat a few minutes later, her nerves taut as she looked down the corridors hoping that, were Lionel to arrive, she might already be safely inside. It seemed an eternity before Julian appeared. He looked flustered and uneasy as he gasped, 'You!'

She hurried past him.

'Close the door,' she commanded, looking through to where Vicky was standing, hair slightly disarrayed, distraught and, it seemed, bewildered.

Julian demanded, 'What *is* this? Why are you here?' His voice was harsh.

Thea unceremoniously reached the sitting room and shot the question at Vicky. 'Do you know that Lionel is here, in Brighton?'

'Lionel?' Vicky showed impatience. 'Of course

he's not; he's in Rome. He telephoned me from there yesterday evening.'

'I've just seen him in a hire car. It's my guess he'll be ringing any minute.' Thea looked from face to face. 'You can't be blind to the implications of *that*!'

Before they had time to answer, the bell rang long and loud.

Thea moved to the door of what was the bedroom.

'I don't want to be seen to begin with,' she announced warningly. 'Better that you hear what he has to say. And then leave things to me.'

Julian looked both angry and confused, but there was no time to argue.

Thea was right; Lionel pushed past him and strode into the sitting room.

'I knew I'd find you here,' he said threateningly. 'I've waited for this moment when I could confront you both. A nice cosy little scene—one of many!'

Julian stood there listening with intense anger and was about to speak when Lionel raised his voice, 'I don't want any lies from you, *Doctor Fraser*,' he said with scorn. 'You've been having an affair with my wife and I'm going to report you to the GMC, and see that you're struck off——ruined. This has been going on since before we went away on that cruise. What did you take me for?' His face flushed as his temper rose. 'You took advantage of your position and of her, relying on women's weakness when it comes to their doctor. The crushes, the intimacy . . . Now I've got the satisfaction of knowing that, even if you had a defence, I'd make sure your name stank. You've accepted my hospitality and abused it, in order to make love to my wife, and I find her here the moment my back's turned!'

For a second there was an unbearable silence and then, suddenly, Thea stood in the doorway, surveying Lionel with icy condemnation, as she said coolly, 'Have you gone mad?' Her poise, the measured tone of her voice, made his mouth fall agape and then give a little gasp as he stared at Thea as though she were a figment of the imagination.

'Vicky,' Thea went on calmly, 'is here because I asked her to come.'

Lionel scoffed, flashing a glance at Julian and then back to Thea, 'Are you in the habit of inviting guests to Dr Fraser's flat? What right——'

Julian tensed, his gaze never leaving Thea's face as she said with telling conviction, having no compunction about the deception, 'The right of a *fiancée*!' The word reverberated like thunder.

'*Fiancée?*' It was a disbelieving, but at the same time shocked, echo.

'Julian and I got engaged yesterday and we wanted Vicky to celebrate with us, particularly as she was alone.'

Lionel spluttered and ended by looking foolish as he made some unintelligible remark.

Vicky had been standing, shaking, beside the sofa and sat down because her legs refused to support her. She felt faint and desolate. The situation was bizarre, but she knew that Thea was determined to save Julian from ruin and that, but for her prompt action, he would have been facing disgrace.

Meanwhile Julian was transfixed, cast for a part he had not even rehearsed and, but for Thea, would now have been at Lionel's mercy.

'I don't believe it!' Lionel shouted.

Julian spoke for the first time, his voice low and warning, the turmoil within him making coherent thought difficult, and words even more so, his position invidious. 'I suggest in future you get your facts right before you start making wild accusations—no matter who may be your proposed victim.'

Lionel snarled, 'You've still been seeing too much of my wife!'

Thea dared not look at Julian lest contempt showed in her eyes. It was like standing on the edge of a precipice. Her heart was thumping; the atmosphere in the room alive with emotion, the warring elements marshalled for destruction. She looked at Vicky's white strained face and prayed she would rise to the occasion, and just then, to Thea's infinite relief, Vicky said with accusing impatience, turning on Lionel, 'I told you Julian was in love with Thea—I *told* you!'

Lionel remembered the occasion when he had planned to go to Rome early in order to practise this ruse.

Vicky went on, 'You've spoilt the evening, insulted Julian, to say nothing of me.' She managed to keep her voice controlled as she thought how carefully she had arranged it and how high her hopes had been. The present situation turned a knife in her heart. Being brought face to face with the possible results of her relationship with Julian, she could only thank God that Thea had intervened. What was Julian thinking, *feeling*, as he stood there, maintaining his control, accepting the situation with an inevitable calm? The facts seemed like ice being poured over her heart. Where would Julian and Thea go from here? She knew Lionel, and while he could do no other than accept the facts as they appeared at the moment, any deviation from the pattern and his suspicions would be revived—she had no illusions on that score. He had lost this battle, but one false move and he could still win the war. He was a stubborn man who never forgot what he conceived to be a wrong, and she knew she had been foolish and indiscreet where Julian was concerned, so that he had justification for his doubts. For a second she escaped into a fantasy world. If Julian would fight, tell Lionel to do his worst; that it didn't matter what the consequences, he would face up to them and take her away from it all if needs be. She was a rich woman and he was, she knew, far from being dependent on his profession alone. The world could be theirs and the choice of a homeland unlimited.

She looked at him—a direct but, without realising it, imploring look behind the façade—as she said, 'I'm sorry to have been responsible for this unpleasant scene. You've looked after me and spared me so much. This is most ungracious repayment.'

Lionel felt uncomfortable, despite his anger.

'In any case,' he said gruffly, 'this sees the end of any professional association.'

Thea realised that Julian had not addressed any re-mark to Vicky personally and it was impossible to tell from his expression what his feelings were. There was a low note of regret, even sadness, as he said, 'I'd have given anything for this not to have happened.'

'I suppose it inflates your ego to have all the women——'

Julian thundered, 'You've said enough! I suggest we end this——this *farce*——'

'I still have a right to object to any kind of contact between you and my wife,' retorted Lionel, raising his voice. 'Perhaps now that you're engaged, you'll behave a little more discreetly,' he finished, congratulating himself on having made a point. He looked at Vicky. 'Now let's go.' He added warningly, 'It's the last time you come here—let that be understood.'

Vicky was crying inside; her heart bruised, depression seeping into her like a heavy sea mist. This was not the end that she had seen to the story and, at that moment, she could not imagine any possible way she could manoeuvre to see Julian, even were Thea prepared for her to do so. Would this mean the end of her and Thea's friendship too? If so, she would miss her desperately. As she reached the door of the flat, Lionel beside her, she felt that her world was crumbling and she was leaving behind everything that made life worth living.

Lionel paused on his way out and looked first at Thea and then at Julian.

'I shall await your marriage with interest,' he said, and there was a gleam in his eyes which Thea felt to be a warning. 'And—' he addressed Thea—'I prefer that you have no further contact with my wife, *Nurse* Craig.' He didn't wait for any comment, but propelled Vicky towards the lifts. She might have been a puppet he was manipulating.

The silence of the flat seemed uncanny as Julian and Thea faced each other. Thea did not know what to expect from him, but was not prepared for his grave dignity as he said, 'I owe you a very great debt.'

Her reply was scornful. 'Did you seriously think you could get away with your relationship with Vicky? That Lionel was blind? Or were you prepared to throw everything away—including your honour as a doctor? Vicky needed someone to protect her, not entice her into what could only be a disastrous affair.'

They faced each other with emotion at its height, tension gripping them so that words became futile; the situation delicate and dangerous as the future had to be discussed, the dark secrets protected, plans made.

'All my sympathies are with Vicky,' Thea burst out in sudden anger. 'She's a loving, *giving* person, and you took a mean advantage. She has an unsatisfactory marriage and you've done your best to wreck it, instead of using your influence for her good. If you call that love—which no doubt you do—I think it's an insult to it . . . To have her here this evening—you, her doctor . . .' She made a little disgusted sound. 'How blantant can you be?' She added, and her words smote him, 'How *cheap*!'

Julian's face became a mask, grim, inscrutable, his voice as sharp as a razor. 'Why did you come here? Make *my* business *yours*?'

Her eyes blazed. 'If you're flattering yourself that I did it for you . . .' emotion almost choked her as she rushed on, letting the words pour out to release her pent-up feelings, 'then you couldn't be more wrong. I did it for Robert—' the name came without conscious thought. 'He's your partner, part of the practice, and its ruin would shatter him. Even in *these* days, being struck off for adultery with a patient isn't regarded lightly.' She never remembered being so angry, or hating anyone so much; hating because she loved him and he was lost to her, the scars of this night to remain for ever, she told herself as she stood there shaking, cold, desperate.

There was what seemed an endless, unendurable silence before Julian said simply, 'I see.'

'Oh God,' she cried, 'I wish you *had*, and then this wreckage would have been spared. Did you even *notice* the look of anguish on Vicky's face? Did it give you a feeling of power? What has she got now?' She waited, hoping he would make some attempt to defend himself, but he deliberately walked to the drinks tray and poured out a whisky and a sherry—the latter he set down on the table beside the chair in which she had almost dropped.

'What you think of me is unimportant,' he said heavily. 'A situation has been created and you've become involved in it. For that I'm deeply sorry.' He drank gratefully from the glass. 'Now we have to decide on the best method——'

Thea cut in, completely commanding, 'We shall remain engaged just as long as I think it necessary to protect your name, which means the practice,' she added. 'And if it involves our ultimately marrying and divorcing, I'd go through with that, too.'

Julian sat down.

'And Robert?'

'Whatever I do, Robert will understand,' Thea insisted. 'You don't imagine he hasn't been aware of your relationship with Vicky?' Frustration mounted. 'I can understand your feelings for her; she's a lovable person, but your folly in having her *here* this evening . . .'

Still he remained silent with neither excuse nor explanation, and her fury increased. And then, suddenly, it struck her that his position was both invidious and intolerable. Silence his only weapon; the sense of loss unbearable as he had seen Vicky walk out of his life. For a second pity stirred and her voice was a trifle more gentle as she went on, 'We shall have to adjust our relationship in public; put an announcement in the newspapers and tell your parents.' She thought of Robert. How easy to say that he would understand, when he was expecting an answer to his proposal on Monday. 'Lionel will watch your every move. He was presented with a *fait accompli*, but that doesn't mean he was convinced by it. On the other hand, it confounded his suspicions.'

Julian's words came with faint cynicism. 'Your acting was flawless. You didn't make the mistake of being effusive where I was concerned.'

She met his gaze for a fleeting second. 'You can count on my never being *that*.' She went on, 'It will be a strain——' then broke off, painfully aware of him. His fiancée . . . associated with him; the fuss, good wishes, congratulations. For the first time she realized the significance of what she had done. What would Trevor say? Pretence would be very difficult where he was concerned. *Pretence*. There was irony in the fact that she was 'engaged' to the man she loved!

Julian sighed deeply, almost painfully.

'I'm desperately sorry,' he muttered, his voice low. 'God knows I didn't foresee this——'

'No,' she retorted, 'for an intelligent man you've been singularly blind.'

He held her gaze masterfully, the atmosphere tense. 'That's the truest word you've uttered.'

'Emotion,' she added, hurting herself with the thought, 'robs us of sanity, unfortunately, or there'd be no tragedies.'

Still Julian unnerved her with his steady scrutiny.

'You must love Robert very deeply.' The words came unexpectedly.

'I do,' she admitted, but they were not talking of the same love. Nevertheless she knew she had been very close to agreeing to marry him, clinging to the belief that his love for her, and their mutual trust and understanding, would deaden and, eventually, kill the madness of her feelings for Julian—feelings that mocked her as she sat there, realising he had feet of clay. When it came to it, what *would* Robert say? Understanding was a big word and much was asked of it.

The telephone rang like an alarm bell, startling both Julian and herself.

Julian said, 'Dr Fraser . . .' and then, alarmed, '*Vicky!*'

'Lionel's having a swim . . . I had to——'

'I can't talk. Please don't ring.' His voice was firm.

The line went dead.

Thea said, 'She must be mad to risk——'

'She's in a highly nervous state,' he cut in.

'Do you wonder at it? Living on a knife-edge—the lies, the deception.' Thea took a deep breath. 'There's a promise I want from you, Julian.' Her voice was commanding. 'I'm not wasting months of my life by being engaged to you, while you risk the future continuing to see Vicky clandestinely. As I've told you, I'd do anything to spare the practice and Robert, but not to perpetuate your relationship with another man's wife. When all this is over, the best thing you can do is to get one of your own,' she finished bitterly.

The silence was icy. Julian broke it with a curt, 'I can give you that promise, I assure you.'

'I won't be trapped, or at your mercy.' The words rushed out.

'Are you not overlooking the fact that it's I who am at *your* mercy?'

Thea lowered her gaze to her hands.

'Don't let's make this more painful than it is,' she whispered, control snapping.

He burst out, 'Oh God, Thea, I'm sorry—you'll never

know how sorry. I've been such a *fool*.' He paused and seemed about to enlarge on the remark, then thought better of it, and said in a forthright fashion, 'You'll need an engagement ring.' With that he disappeared and after a minute or so returned with a case which revealed a flawless diamond set with three smaller ones on either side. 'This belonged to my maternal aunt,' he said. 'I'd like you to keep it.'

'I will wear it,' she agreed, 'but not keep it. We have nothing to give each other, you and I.' As she spoke, a lump rose in her throat, emotion overwhelmed her as she slipped the ring on her finger, aching to be in his arms. Nothing could assuage that desire, or the longing he awakened; not his defects, or his love for Vicky. If, she thought cynically, you could call it love. *Please don't ring*. She could feel the agony that those three words would cause Vicky and, even in the circumstances, wished she might offer some palliative. But contact was too dangerous, and she knew it was a chapter that had to come to this cruel end. Was Julian relieved? Was he such a coward when it came to it that his lucky escape had dulled any regrets he might otherwise have felt at their parting? Who could tell: he was as inscrutable now as on the day she had first met him.

The telephone rang again. Her gaze met his, mutely enquiring if she should answer it.

'I'll take it,' he said with the command of a man prepared to face up to any situation. Then, 'Robert!' There was relief and welcome in the sound. 'Oh—Mrs Gerrard. Yes, transfer to me. 'Bye.' He replaced the receiver and turned to Thea. 'Mrs Gerrard's had a fall. Robert needs me to take the calls.'

Thea merely nodded. She felt almost guilty being with

Julian in circumstances to which Robert was not privy. She got to her feet and Julian said as she picked up her handbag, 'I'll tell Robert about all this if you like. I don't want to be shielded any more than is necessary in the circumstances.'

Thea spoke to him over her shoulder as she went out of the room.

'I'm afraid that's part of the price you'll have to pay. I prefer to tell Robert myself,' she said firmly. 'I'll get in touch with him tomorrow. Miss Jenkins and Enid will have a shock . . . I'm seeing Trevor tomorrow lunchtime and shall tell him, too. I shall say you're busy. I couldn't stand having you there.'

Julian opened the front door for her, but he didn't speak.

Thea telephoned Robert early on Sunday morning and he arrived at her flat, as arranged, at ten-thirty, his excitement tempered with apprehension as he saw her strained face.

'Something's wrong,' he said intuitively. 'You're not going to say "yes".'

'I don't really know what I'm going to say,' she confessed. 'I know I've said I could tell you anything, but this is such a——'

'You're going to marry Julian.' The words came sharply and with a degree of disgust.

'No,' she corrected, 'that's the last thing.'

'Then nothing else matters,' he exclaimed promptly.

When it came to it Thea hated what could only be a betrayal of Julian; yet she owed Robert the truth, not just as a safeguard and explanation, but because of their personal relationship.

'If it were as simple as that!'

They had been standing in her sunlit sitting room and suddenly, weakly, she sat down, indicating a coffee-pot and cups on a nearby tray. He acted on her mute appeal and poured it out, setting her cup on a side table by her chair and then sitting down immediately opposite her.

'Plain facts, please, Thea. Whatever it is.'

She took a deep breath, sipped her coffee and told him the whole story, to which he listened with only one or two exclamations, his expression becoming grimmer as she finished with, 'I could think of no other way of silencing Lionel.'

His reaction was solely personal.

'Your protective instinct towards Julian must be very strong for you to go to such lengths to save his reputation.'

The truth served.

'I didn't allow him to have that comfort. I said I was doing it for you and the practice.'

'And were you?' His voice was sharp.

'Yes,' she replied, adding, 'but that doesn't automatically exclude Julian.'

'The man's a fool!' said Robert, his voice raised. 'I suspected there was something, but as long as he didn't start attracting you . . . I've had some bad moments, particularly when you went to the Grand that night . . . He knows you're going to tell me?'

Thea explained that Julian was more than prepared to explain the situation himself.

Robert leaned forward and let his hands drop between his knees in a rather helpless fashion.

'And where do you and he go from here?'

Thea's heart quickened its beat.

'Nowhere,' she said flatly. 'The engagement will serve a purpose and be broken when it's safe to do so. It will be strictly for the benefit of outsiders.'

'I hate it,' he muttered.

'Not so much as I do,' she said honestly, telling herself that she was going to build up a wall of enmity, strengthened by the knowledge of Vicky's suffering for which he was responsible. Curiously enough she could feel only pity for Vicky. Her pathetic insistence to Lionel that Julian was in love with her, Thea, emphasised the lengths to which she had gone to protect the secrecy of the liaison. Thea saw again the clasped hands that night in the swimming pool, and heard Vicky's *'Darling!'* at the hospital. How many times had she secretly been to Julian's flat? . . . The telephone calls and visits . . . Had he been innocent, he would have ceased to be in any professional association with her, even as he had originally mooted. When it came to it . . . She broke off. It was so easy to be strong for other people. Had Julian seriously made love to her, Thea, would she have been able to resist him? Now it was different. Her resentment and anger deadened emotion the more she dwelt on the situation. She looked at Robert and felt a surge of respect and affection, deep, inescapable. Her admiration for him made their relationship special, and never more so than at that moment.

He said suddenly and without dramatics, 'Lionel can't hold a threat over Julian indefinitely. His relationship with his wife is the vital issue. He can bring a case as and when he wishes if she doesn't placate him. Whichever way you look at it, Julian is at his mercy. So Julian might win in a divorce action, but it would be a most unpleasant business.' He stopped. 'No matter how one argues, the reconciliation and survival of that marriage is the king-pin in all this.'

'You mean one false move on Vicky's part——'

'Just that. There's nothing vicious or evil about her; but she's weak, emotional, and must be deeply in love with Julian. I've always felt that.'

'Then,' Thea said involuntarily, 'she would want to protect him.'

Robert shook his head.

'What one wants to do and what one *does* . . . so far she hasn't been exactly discreet, any more than he has. She's a very highly strung person who doesn't really trust herself.'

'We can only take it one day at a time,' Thea said fearfully.

'And I can only wait,' came the tense reply.

Thea looked at him regretfully. 'I'm sorry, Robert. There's nothing I'd like more than to be able to say I love you and will marry you next week.' She stopped. 'I feel I'm in an emotional spin-dryer. I'm tied.'

'Which is a form of escape and protection,' he reminded her. 'Julian is my partner and my friend, but I've never felt more animosity towards him than at this moment. I shan't spare him when I have this out with him, I assure you.' He broke off, then, 'Does Trevor know?'

Thea lowered her gaze. She did not underestimate what it would cost her to pretend and she dreaded having to tell him that lunchtime.

'I've got to convince him of my happiness—only that will matter to him.'

Suddenly Robert said belligerently, 'I shall expect our friendship to go on as usual.'

There was a moment's silence.

'That won't be possible. I'll have to behave like an engaged girl, or this would be to no avail. Gossip about my friendship with you would endanger the whole situation.'

'I shall telephone,' he insisted, 'and include myself in some of your social events.' There was a note of bitterness in his voice.

'*Please*,' she appealed to him. 'I can't fight on two fronts. Without your support I don't know what I'd do.'

'Really?' He brightened.

The front door bell rang, and Thea jumped, startled. It was Julian.

'I'm sorry to disturb you,' he said, 'but——'

Robert, hearing his voice, came out into the hall.

'I was going to get in touch with you,' he said coldly. 'What I have to say can just as well be said here.'

Thea made a gesture to invite Julian in. He looked strained, and she wondered if he had managed to contact Vicky in some way.

Julian looked from face to face as they reached the sitting room.

'I can spare you the vituperation,' he exclaimed. 'The situation is not made any more bearable because I'm aware of my own folly. If you, in due course, want to sever our partnership, I shall quite understand.' He spoke with a quiet dignity that made Thea tremble. She could imagine what it must be costing him to face up to the truth.

The remark arrested the angry words Robert was about to utter.

'Friendship is made of sterner stuff.' Robert's loyalty was uppermost. 'I don't think any good purpose is to be served by discussing the matter. Thea's told me all that happened last evening, and it's now a question of how soon you can safely release her from this unwarranted obligation.'

Julian took that without wincing. He might have been a stone monument. No emotion betrayed itself on his face, or even in his eyes.

'If Lionel were a man one could reason with——' Julian began, his voice controlled.

'Good God!' Robert cut in, 'a man doesn't *reason* about the infidelity of his wife! Or have you lost all sensitivity?'

A flicker of anger betrayed itself as Julian suggested, 'Anything that lies within my power to enable this *engagement*——' a note of cynicism crept into his voice —'to be broken, I will do. I appreciate how insufferable the idea of it is and the sacrifices that will be entailed.'

In that moment Thea asked herself if it wouldn't have been better had she kept out of the situation and let events take their course. But the words, '*struck off*', drummed in her head and she knew the possibility was unthinkable.

Robert said, his attitude serious, 'My relationship with Thea will not be affected—I may as well warn you. Within the bounds of discretion, of course.'

Silence fell, tense, warring.

Julian broke it by saying significantly, 'I understand.'

Thea flushed. She knew Robert had intended to convey more to Julian than was, in fact, true. She did nothing to correct the impression. It strengthened her position.

'And now,' she said, 'why are you here?' She nerved herself to meet his gaze.

'Because I feel it would be most ungracious not to accompany you to Trevor's this lunchtime. Normally I'd have had the courtesy to tell him my intentions, had we wished to become engaged. As it is . . . we don't want any stress for him, any worries. It's essential for his health that we——'

'Put on a good act,' Thea said.

Robert exclaimed, 'Julian has a point. Did you wish to go alone?' He looked at Thea.

'Yes.' It was almost curt. 'I didn't stop to think.' She sighed. 'Very well,' she spoke brusquely to Julian, 'we'll meet there at twelve-thirty.'

Julian inclined his head and moved towards the door.

'I'm sorry to have disturbed you,' he said. 'I can see myself out.'

Later, Thea drove to the Royal Crescent to find Julian awaiting her. She had put on her ring which sparkled in the bright afternoon sun. The day was fine; people were leisurely walking along Marine Parade, and the sea was dotted with small craft bobbing up and down on its choppy waters. She noticed Julian was wearing an oat-meal jacket and beige trousers, looking smart and attractive, but very grave. For a second she allowed herself to imagine what he must be feeling; how his world must have fallen apart, and the drama of this moment must bring unbearable depression.

'Trevor's up on the balcony, looking down on us,' she said swiftly. 'He isn't expecting you . . . I wish I could think of something funny to take the funereal look off our faces——'

'I shall have to call you "darling",' Julian said irrelevantly.

Thea laughed mirthlessly. 'At least that *is* funny in the circumstances!'

'I'm so deeply sorry you've been dragged into this,' he said heavily.

'So am I,' she agreed, 'but I have only myself to blame.'

'And I,' he said almost impatiently, as though he could not bear the knowledge of his own actions.

Suddenly, with a rush of compassion for which she despised herself, she said, 'This has got to be endured, Julian. Let's go through with it in a civilised fashion. It's essential we don't invite conjecture, otherwise nothing will have been achieved and Lionel will triumph at your expense. His suspicions are very deep-rooted.' She found her voice trembling. 'We weren't enemies before, and I'll do my best to prevent our becoming so now. Trevor must not suspect, or know, until such time as we're free to tell him. We can only await events.'

'Thank you,' Julian said quietly.

Thea felt a strange depression. Freedom would write *finis* to their relationship.

Trevor accepted the news with only Thea's happiness uppermost in his mind. He had hoped that Robert might have been the stabilising influence and become his future son-in-law, since Howard had dropped out of the picture, while never losing sight of the fact that Julian was a highly attractive man by whom women were fascinated—the more so since he was a doctor. Thea's emotions, however, were difficult to assess and he could never come to any definite conclusion as to where her affections might lie. The thought of Robert induced a sadness. He would be bereft.

Thea played her part with skill. Trevor kissed her and said, 'All I want is your happiness.' He shook Julian's hand. 'Take care of her.' He smiled knowingly. 'She's a little wild and unpredictable!'

'Facts that haven't escaped me,' Julian managed to say indulgently.

'With Julian's inscrutability we should be a riot!' Thea exclaimed, telling herself there was nothing to arouse any apprehension where Trevor was concerned. She knew, nevertheless, that Trevor had Robert in mind, without the fact causing her anxiety. She accepted Trevor's words, 'All I want is your happiness', and knew that the sentiment would apply even if he had been unsympathetic towards her choice of a husband.

'This calls for champagne,' said Trevor a minute or two later, and went into the kitchen to ask Mrs Kingsley to bring in the glasses. He always kept some champagne in a cooler and got out a bottle of Bollinger with a feeling of occasion.

When Mrs Kingsley, a slim, quiet and shy woman of sixty-two, brought in the tray and glasses, Trevor said, 'You must stay and have a celebration drink with us. We've got an engagement on our hands!'

Mrs Kingsley, part of the family, looked from Thea to Julian and gave a little gasp of surprise. She had rather thought of Dr Robert, but managed to conceal her reactions and offer her good wishes and congratulations. A second or two later she and Trevor raised their glasses. A toast was drunk.

Julian and Thea stood side by side and joined in the drinking, looking at each other and then lowering their gaze.

'A short engagement,' Trevor suggested.

'It hasn't been discussed yet, but I hope so,' said Julian, and his voice rang with sincerity.

It was, Thea thought, the height of irony that Julian was thinking in terms of freedom, Trevor of marriage. With a firm resolve she said, to Julian's amazement, 'I second that, and suggest the end of the year.'

CHAPTER NINE

THE TRUCE held between Julian and Thea, and July and August faded into September, Brighton and Hove taking to themselves a peaceful dignity reminiscent of Regency days, the Nash terraces beautified by the long shadows that crept stealthily upon their elegant façades.

There was one dramatic occasion during that time when they came face to face with Lionel and Vicky at a concert held at the Royal Pavilion, and Thea was afraid Vicky was going to faint. Lionel glowered without speaking, and Thea knew his jealousy still festered, his suspicions remained. He propelled Vicky forward in exactly the same way as he had done at the flat on that last momentous occasion.

Thea had remained silent where Vicky was concerned, and had received no word from her. The dangers were too great, and Thea was thankful that Vicky had the good sense to realise it. Julian had not mentioned Vicky's name and made no comment after their meeting. It was, Thea, thought, like a film or TV play in which she was an actress who had not been given her lines and recognised only the character she was intended to play.

On this particular morning, Robert had invited her and Julian to the Old Ship Hotel for dinner, maintaining that they had not got together for far too long. Neither Thea nor Julian had time to consider the idea seriously, and suggested they discuss it later. Robert strode off, ill-tempered—an extremely unusual reaction.

'I've a case I'd like to discuss before we really start,' said Thea, looking at Julian a trifle anxiously. 'Can you spare a moment?'

'Certainly.' During the past weeks, Julian had been both polite and even-tempered, his mood not varying, almost as though he had become a machine set to function at a given number.

'It's Mrs Fellows——'

'The infertility couple?' He looked surprised. He was dealing with her and her husband, and could find no reason why Thea should be consulted, but he said carefully, 'Perhaps there's something she doesn't want to confide to me.'

'I just wanted to put you in the picture.'

He held her gaze.

'You've never forgiven me over the Manfield case, have you?' His voice was low and the words tentative.

Thea exclaimed, 'Forgiveness doesn't come into it—I try not to make the same mistake twice.' She added swiftly, 'The last thing we want is any professional disagreement.'

'I wonder just how much you'd be prepared to forgive a person?'

'That would depend on their behaviour, rather than the crime! But we haven't time to go into that . . . I'll hear what Mrs Fellows has to say.'

'Do; and if there's anything I should know, put me wise.'

She left him and went into her office where Enid was attending to the early post. The atmosphere in the practice had subtly changed since the engagement. Enid had said only that morning to Miss Jenkins, 'If you ask me, there's something strange about Dr Fraser and Nurse Craig.'

'No one *is* asking you,' came the acid reply. 'It's not your business.'

'Which means you agree with me . . . take the case of the Holfords, whipping away their case notes and changing to Dr Lawson—after all Dr Fraser did for her, too.' Enid paused and gave a little giggle. 'She'd got a crush on him all right, and he——'

'That,' said Miss Jenkins, removing her glasses and putting them back again, without reason, 'is quite enough. Get on with your work.'

Enid smirked and then said goodnaturedly, 'All right. He's *perfect*!' She swung out of the room before any more could be said.

Thea was grateful to be dealing with Mrs Fellows. She made a change from the routine checks that went on *ad infinitum*, and there was something in Mrs Fellows' manner that suggested nervous tension and fear.

'I feel stupid,' she began without preliminaries. 'Mark, my husband, and I have been coming to Dr Fraser because we can't have children—I'm not to blame. We've had all the tests, to find out if it's poor egg production, rejection of sperm, blockage between sperm and egg—I can appreciate all this, but now that we're dealing with artificial insemination——'

'AIH,' Thea prompted.

'Yes. I don't need a donor. But Dr Fraser talks of our being able to do the insemination ourselves. He only spoke of it in passing last time we saw him, but my mind wasn't functioning and, just as I don't ask the right questions, I also don't hear what he's really saying!' She made a helpless gesture. 'Why—*why* do apparently intelligent people become morons when faced by a perfectly normal human being called a doctor? You go to him knowing the questions you want to ask and that are vital: you come away not having asked them. He tells you to take two pills three times a day and you think he's said take three pills twice a day!' She forced a little nervous laugh. 'Dr Fraser is most helpful and *asks* if there are any questions. When he does that, my mind goes a complete blank!'

Thea laughed. 'If I had the answer I'd be the most sought-after nurse in the town,' she exclaimed. 'But AIH is perfectly simple. It has to be done at the exact time of the menstrual cycle when the egg is being made. You've obviously had all the preliminary investigations. It's merely a matter of giving you a plastic syringe and showing you how to use it, thus your husband's sperm will be transferred, and it's a much more personal and intimate procedure than in the cold clinical atmosphere of a hospital.'

'Oh, I see.' Mrs Fellows sighed with relief. 'We've been dealing with premature ejaculation among other things, so that procedure should be easy . . . We're very happy, Mark and I, but we both long for children, or *a* child. I've adjusted to the sexual side of our life——' She spoke without embarrassment. 'Mark and I have everything in common—humour, the same interests—a child would complete——' Her voice broke slightly, but she managed to smile through her glistening eyes as she added, 'Sorry to get emotional. You've been so understanding——' She broke off again. 'Neither Mark nor I like the idea of AID. A "donor" sounds so cold and clinical, and it wouldn't be the same——'

'That's why doing the insemination yourselves makes it all more personal.'

'And if we failed? Or didn't do it right?' Mrs Fellows looked forlorn, 'We've waited six years.'

'Then it could always be done professionally. Dr Faser will explain it. It's a good idea to write your questions down and hand him the paper—saves time and frustration,' Thea said with a little smile.

'Doctors must think their patients are awfully stupid.'

Thea laughed outright. 'Sometimes; but they understand all that I've been saying to you.'

'Will you have a talk to him before we see him? My husband's joining me here at eleven.'

'Of course, if you wish.'

'You and he are engaged,' came the somewhat awed remark. Mrs Fellows had great respect for the medical profession.

'Yes.' Thea looked down at her ringless hand. 'I can't wear my ring at this job, or I'd wash it away.'

'No; of course. Ah, well, that won't apply to your wedding ring!' She looked at Thea intently. 'Marriage is wonderful if you really love each other. You can fight through anything.'

As Thea heard the words, a little wave of sickness went over her. Mrs Fellows had just emphasised what a sham her own life was.

Julian listened attentively to what Thea had to tell him a short while later.

'I thought I'd explained,' he remarked.

'Mechanical things don't register—neither does the unfamiliar.'

'That's true. Thank you.' His voice was smooth. It was

amazing how they had established a formal distant attitude without animosity. 'Tell Enid I'm free. Oh,' as Thea reached the door of his room, 'how do you feel about Robert's invitation?'

'That I'd like to accept it,' she said firmly.

'A means of getting through another evening,' came the unexpected comment.

'Exactly.' Her voice was distant. He was speaking for himself, she thought bitterly, and realised anew what a stranger he was. The thought of Vicky came sharply. His loyalty and fidelity to her were phenomenal.

'Some time, we could go to the Royal Pavilion to the Regency Exhibition. I love looking at the Regency silver, glass and porcelain,' she said in a rush, a certain nervousness making her almost shy as she was aware of his intense gaze.

'Anything you like,' he agreed. 'And we could go to a concert at the Dome. It's a pretty impressive concert hall——'

'It closes at six-thirty in September,' she reminded him.

'A Saturday——'

She nodded, gave the message to Enid and went back to the patients. The snatched few moments served to remind her how precarious their relationship was, and the time factor hazardous.

It was when the day was nearly over, the last patient gone, the waiting room empty, that Julian paused in the doorway of Miss Jenkins' office. Enid and Thea were gathered there, discussing the day's work.

'A last cup of coffee?' suggested Enid, judging his mood. It was rarely he had time for small talk.

'Why not?' he said. 'Thank you.'

She turned swiftly and went into the common room, immediately bringing one back.

'I'd just made it,' she said with a grin.

'I thought that was a bit prompt—even for you,' Julian smiled. 'No one else?' He looked at Thea.

The front door opened and shut heavily, and Robert appeared, shaken, pale.

'You haven't heard?'

'What?' Julian was instantly alert.

'Vicky—Vicky Holford. An accident! Her car went over the cleft at the Devil's Dyke. I heard it just now on the local radio . . . She's dead!'

There was a second of horrified silence before Julian exclaimed, 'Oh, my God—no!' His voice was hollow, his expression stricken.

'But when did it happen?' Miss Jenkins asked in a breath.

'There was only a brief announcement.'

Thea went icy cold, her skin seeming to lift from her flesh. What dread secret would this reveal, and what revenge would Lionel take if there should be anything suspicious about the circumstances?

Enid, forthright and not prone to tact, cried, 'Wouldn't it be awful if it were suicide? She was a very highly-strung type.'

Robert said with authority, 'Suppose we avoid adding to the drama. It's tragic enough.'

Still Julian had only uttered that first exclamation. Now he said, 'I've a letter to write. We can only wait for further news.' He looked at Thea; in the space of a few seconds their respective lives had changed.

Thea mentally visualised the Devil's Dyke, a vast Vshaped chasm in the Downs, south of Fulking, on the road out of Brighton, which gave long panoramic views across the Weald. She recalled Vicky telling her that according to legend, the gap had been made by the Devil who, in order to combat the growth of Christianity, started to dig a trench through which the English Channel would flood the Weald. A woman watching him held up a candle and the Devil fled, mistaking it for the rising sun.

She said involuntarily, 'Vicky loved that spot. She so often went there.' Her gaze met Julian's.

Enid gave a little shudder. 'It doesn't bear thinking about!'

They dispersed. Julian went alone to his room, while Robert followed Thea into her office.

'I suppose I did that clumsily,' he said ruefully. 'I should have waited to tell Julian on his own.'

'I don't think it matters,' she said in a dead voice.

'This will change the situation.' He could not keep the note of hope from his voice.

'That depends on what emerges. Death sometimes has an unfortunate way of dragging skeletons from cupboards.'

'Would you still stand by him?'

'The motives wouldn't alter. It just doesn't seem *possible*.'

'Strange,' Robert mused, 'we live with death, yet it's always a shock.' He added, 'I can't help feeling sorry for Julian. It must have hit him hard, no matter what happened in the past.' He was watching Thea carefully as he spoke.

The nerves in Thea's stomach seemed to be frayed; a hollow emptiness added to the sensation. Her thoughts were in chaos. Enid's words, '*Wouldn't it be awful if it were suicide?*' struck terror into her heart, and her own reactions matched the fear.

'I've got to have a word with him,' she said abruptly. 'And, Robert——'

'Yes?' It was a crisp, faintly suspicious sound.

'About this evening . . .'

'You want to put it off?'

'I was fond of Vicky,' she said simply. 'A question of moods.'

'You're thinking of *him* . . . but I see your point. Conversation could be rather tricky, with just the three of us.'

'Exactly. It isn't a question of morbidity.'

Julian was sitting with his elbows on his desk, chin cupped in hands, and he didn't change the posture as Thea knocked and heard his 'Come in'. It almost seemed that he hadn't the energy, or will, to do so. He looked at her with directness and indicated the patients' chair. She sat down in silence. It was a strange silence that held all the drama of events without any alleviation. Vicky was dead, and she seemed more alive at that moment than when she had been among them.

He said, without preliminaries, 'Just as long as it wasn't *suicide*——' The stricken look on his face smote her, and she could not challenge him with either anger or accusation.

'It was a favourite spot of hers. I remember that day,' Thea reflected, 'when we three met in Hannington's; she talked of wanting to be there, and people not having time to——' Her voice broke.

'I remember,' he said dully.

'We shan't know until the inquest.'

Eyes met eyes, apprehension casting its shadow.

'No.'

'I'm glad it's public that we're to be married at the end of the year,' Thea exclaimed.

Julian said, 'You're free, Thea. You always have been, of course; but now——' He broke off.

There was an awkward silence before she said, 'Even so, we mustn't precipitate a crisis by breaking the "engagement",' there was a gentle irony in her voice, 'before everything is settled. A wrong move now, when we don't know what lies ahead——' Emotion overwhelmed her, 'I can't believe it's happened!'

'The thing is *how* she died.'

Thea sensed that the manner of Vicky's death was even more vital to Julian than the fact of her dying. Was that guilt? The feeling that he had contributed towards the tragedy in the event of it being suicide? Why couldn't he confide the dark secret that obviously haunted him; why was everything emotional concealed? She wanted to question, to understand, half of her compassionate, half resentful and suspicious.

'Only time and the inquest will reveal that,' she said solemnly, wondering if he was thinking of the last words he had uttered to Vicky: *'Please don't ring'*. Yet how did she know that he had not maintained some secret contact in the meantime? It was like walking in the dark through a curtain of cobwebs.

He made a sound on the edge of a deep sigh.

'I've put off the meal with Robert tonight,' she told him a few seconds later.

He looked relieved.

'I'm grateful.' It struck her that his behaviour was uninhibited and as if he expected his grief to be taken for granted. 'What are *you* going to do?'

That told her he wanted to be alone, and slight irritation made her say a trifle curtly, 'Go to see Trevor. He'll be shocked—if he's heard the news.'

'He will have,' Julian insisted. 'Tragedy travels on the wind.'

'Lionel,' Thea exclaimed suddenly, 'will be desolate —a terrible ordeal to have to face.'

Their gazes met and fell away. Julian didn't speak. Tension built up as he moved from his desk towards her chair. 'You're a tower of strength, Thea,' he said unexpectedly and irrelevantly.

The local morning papers—and several of the London—carried news of the tragedy, seemingly in accord, as they stressed that Mrs Holford was accustomed to picnicking at that particular spot. She had been trapped in the car which had not yet been recovered; but it was understood that a letter and several postcards, already stamped, had been found inside it. She had been looking forward to a holiday on the Orient Express, leaving in a few days' time. There was nothing to suggest foul play, or that it was other than an accident. Lionel Holford's position was emphasised, also that he had a large house in The Drive, Hove. An atmosphere of luxury was created.

'It doesn't look as though there's any suspicion of suicide,' Robert said firmly, having a word with Thea between patients. 'Thank God for that!'

Julian heard the words as he joined them in passing on his way to a midder.

'Thank God for what?'

Robert repeated his words.

'I agree,' said Julian, a shadow crossing his face.

'Nothing else is important,' he added on a note of desperation of which he was unaware. 'I'll be at Mrs Summers,' he said, looking at Thea.

'I know . . . I took the call. This will be her fifth.'

He straightened himself as though returning to reality.

Robert said when he was gone, 'This has hit him badly. When you come to think of it——'

'I've got work to do,' Thea said abruptly. 'And so have you.' She looked at Robert admonishingly.

'I'm aware of that,' he retorted. 'You do realise that you're free?'

'I realise only that I have a patient waiting,' she retorted, and went to her desk, flicking the intercom switch with an air of dismissal so far as Robert was concerned.

The following evening, Julian and Thea had a quiet meal together at her flat, and at nine o'clock, Julian said, 'I'll get back now. I've a case I want to read up . . .' He met her gaze and her expression told him that she realised his anxiety.

'It's rather ironical that, while we're free,' she said, 'it would be very indiscreet if we were publicly to break off our engagement. It would emphasise to Lionel that it had been a sham and that he'd been right. I wonder, now, what his attitude would be?'

Julian stiffened, his expression darkened. 'I'm sorry to keep you tied; it must be infuriating.'

'I've used the word many times before. *Ironical* fits the situation. Time solves most problems. I can keep up the pretence if you can!'

He drew her gaze to his and emotion surged between them.

'Why not?' His voice was low and she thrilled to its depth.

'Good night, Julian,' she said with sudden dismissal, her nerves raw, desire like a fire within her, the situation a scourge.

He walked to the door and turned back to look at her, 'Good night, Thea. I'm sorry I've caused you so much annoyance.' And with that he went to the front door and let himself out.

The telephone was ringing when he reached his flat.

He gave a deep sigh, then said, 'Dr Fraser.'

'Can I come over to see you—now?' Lionel spoke urgently.

CHAPTER TEN

Lionel stood motionless at the door when Julian answered his ring, then he said, meeting Julian's gaze, 'I had to come.'

Julian looked at him and saw a man who had aged ten years or more. No word was spoken as Julian admitted him and they walked into the sitting room. Julian gave him a brandy without enquiring what he would have to drink. They sat down in the deep armchairs opposite each other.

'I owe you an apology,' Lionel began. 'This tragedy ——' He added, his voice breaking, 'I owe *her* an apology. Her death has put everything into perspective and left me——' He couldn't finish the sentence.

The silence of the room was heavy and seemed to echo with the angry voices raised on the last occasion Lionel was there.

'We don't know what the verdict will be,' Lionel went on disjointedly. He darted a glance at Julian, half appealing, half apologetic. 'You wouldn't have any ideas? I mean——'

'None, I'm afraid,' Julian said with a quiet conviction. 'The shock——'

'If there were any questions . . . I don't know about these things. My solicitor seems to think it will be accidental death . . . I dread the inquest.' Lionel made a helpless gesture. 'If you should be called—if——'

'Whatever I could do to help, but I haven't been in the

picture, and Dr Lawson would be of greater assistance if it came to establishing her state of mind.'

'I thought she was going to have a nervous breakdown after that night—but she didn't. She suddenly seemed to look at everything differently. We've been happier these past months than ever before in our marriage. She even convinced me that she loved me. What the papers say is true: we were going on that holiday—the Orient Express; everything was fixed . . . and we'd planned to have another child—a second-honeymoon child.'

Julian murmured under his breath, 'Thank God!' but Lionel didn't hear him, he was living in his own particular hell and had come to Julian as he might have gone to a priest to ease his conscience. He burst out, 'We don't realise that when a person dies, suddenly everything ever said is magnified, and one blames oneself even for innocent remarks. I was too jealous to be rational and I caused her hell at times. That haunts me . . .'

'The only thing that's important,' Julian said quietly, 'is your recent happiness together. Remember that, instead of tormenting yourself over the past.'

'I was prepared to ruin you; determined to do so, in fact.'

Julian looked at him steadily. 'I'm fully aware of that.'

'I owe you an apology, as I've already said . . . that night in this room. If it hadn't been for your engagement I'd have smashed everything.' Lionel looked at Julian as though the past tormented him still. 'You're being married at the end of the year, I understand?'

'As things stand.'

'I ought to have believed Vicky about you and Thea——'

Julian said suddenly, 'Look here, Lionel, none of this

is of help. You tell me you'd never been happier and that everything looked bright, in effect, for the future. Dwell on that, otherwise it isn't much of a compliment to—to Vicky, is it?' He finished, his voice faintly critical, 'Neither does it make your apology to me very acceptable.'

Lionel shook his head.

'I don't seem to be able to hold one mood for long. When I get my thoughts adjusted and coherent, some unpleasant memory cuts across it all, and fear takes away any calm.'

Julian sympathised. God knew, he understood.

'There's something I want to ask you.' The words came abruptly.

Julian tensed. 'And that is?'

'Have you seen Vicky since that night here?'

'Only on the occasion when Thea and I met you both at the Royal Pavilion.'

Lionel looked sheepish and a little awkward. 'Forgive me; I see shadows where none exist. My nerves are in a hellish state. Perhaps I shouldn't have come. I don't seem to be making a very good job of it.'

'I understand,' said Julian quietly.

'Do you happen to know if—if Thea has seen her?'

Julian didn't hesitate. 'I'm sure she hasn't, or she would have told me.'

'I was harsh over Thea. I know Vicky missed her.' Lionel made a desperate gesture. 'I live with guilt at every turn; something I ought to have done and didn't, or the other way round.' He paused as though hoping Julian would speak of the past, but Julian did no more than comment on Lionel's observations without making any of his own. At no time did he give him the consolation of suggesting that there had never been any relationship whatsoever between himself and Vicky, and that Lionel's suspicions and convictions had no foundation in fact.

Julian asked the question that had been uppermost in his mind. 'Is there any theory as to how the accident could have happened?'

Lionel looked shattered. 'The possibility that she put her foot on the accelerator instead of the brake. It was a new car—an automatic—which she'd hardly driven. She specially wanted it. She was—' the past tense made him pause and his voice broke slightly as he added, 'she was a good driver, but she could be reckless.'

Julian relaxed slightly. There was obviously no suggestion of suicide in Lionel's mind, or the possibility of any other tragedy.

Lionel looked him straight in the eyes.

'I'm sorry . . . but have you telephoned or written to Vicky since——'

Julian's voice was icy and resounding. 'I've had no contact whatsoever . . . your attitude is very strange for a man who speaks of having been so happy recently.'

Lionel's hands were clenched.

'I know.' It was an admission of weakness. 'But the stress and the grief——'

Julian nodded and sighed. He wanted Lionel to leave; his presence brought back the drama of that night. And as if sensing Julian's mood, Lionel got to his feet.

'I hope you'll be very happy in your marriage. But for your engagement—I owe everything to that.'

'Good night,' Julian said somewhat dismissively. And as he saw Lionel out and returned to the sitting room, it struck him that Lionel's reactions to the tragedy were more embroiled with the old suspicions than with the mourning and momentousness of that which lay ahead. Restlessly, he looked at the clock. It was nine-thirty. He dialled Thea's number.

'Is it too late for me to come to see you?' he asked.

Thea said, 'I've just showered and I'm in my house-coat . . . Has something happened?' There was fear in her voice.

'No.' He decided not to tell her of Lionel's visit, which would inevitably revive the past, and was the last thing he wanted.

Thea didn't change out of her attractive cream-and-turquoise brocade housecoat, which emphasised her perfect figure. As she admitted Julian the faint subtle Stanley Hall scent, *Zara*, clung to her warm body and wafted delicately in the air, and it seemed that they had stepped into a private world where only emotion had any meaning. Without a word being uttered, his arms went around her and his lips parted hers in a deep passionate kiss. She clung to him, heart thudding, and then, breath-less, she drew back, staggered, only her eyes, dark, questioning, meeting his almost in appeal, love over-whelming her as his deep voice whispered, 'If you knew how I wanted to do that . . . you must have *known*.'

Thea looked amazed and almost disbelieving.

'That's the last thing to have occurred to me in the circumstances,' she managed to say, trying to regain her composure. A nervous tension built up within her. When it came to it, was Julian the kind of man to make love to her, despite the present tragedy and all that had gone before with Vicky? If so, then she despised him —and herself, for responding to his kiss in such obvious fashion. She tried to release herself from the power of his attraction; to gain sufficient control to resist any further demonstrations; but he moved away from her as he exclaimed, 'Circumstances don't change love!'

There was a tense silence which she broke by echoing in amazement, '*Love*? I don't follow.'

Julian held her gaze with a deep penetrating look. 'I'm in love with you . . . I realised it when you claimed to be engaged to me, although I'd suspected . . . Now I'm asking you to marry me—the pretence over. The tragedy of Vicky's death has forced home the folly of wasting precious days, living a lie, putting on an act.'

She stared at him, his boldness disturbing as she reflected anew on the situation. He went closer to her, putting his hands on her shoulders. She had lowered her gaze and he drew it mesmerically back to his. 'If you can tell me you don't love me, then——' His grip tightened. 'Look at me, Thea. Can you tell me that?'

She was lost, emotion gripping her, the truth clamouring for expression as her voice, low and passionate, murmured, 'No; no, I can't tell you that——'

'And it wasn't for Robert that you fought to save the practice?'

Thea shook her head. 'I had to pretend,' she admitted, 'because I should have betrayed my feelings otherwise.'

'Oh, my *darling*!' His lips came down on hers, his arms enfolding her in a suffocating embrace as his kiss awakened swift desire, bodies tensing, their need almost unendurable as his hands caressed her.

Thea was swirled into an unreal world where the past was lost and problems were non-existent. Only one thing mattered in that moment: Julian loved her—*loved* her; and as she pressed her face against his shoulder and his grip tightened until she was breathless, she cried, 'If only I'd *known*!' She released herself from his grasp and sat down weakly on the sofa. He remained standing, suddenly looking grave.

'There is the past,' she said quietly. 'Love doesn't miraculously alter facts.'

'No,' he agreed, his expression solemn. 'But I'm afraid you'll have to take that on trust.'

She stared at him, her lips parting, her eyes clouding. 'But——'

'I can't tell you the details of my relationship with Vicky. The secrets must die with her. If you don't love me enough to accept that and trust me . . . I shall understand——' His voice was uneven, strain telling on him.

'It's a very great deal to ask,' Thea said without seeking to minimise the gravity. 'Secrets are like shadows that you can't wipe out at will.'

'I can give you my word that I'm not ashamed of my relationship with Vicky.'

'But you admit it was a relationship?' The words came swiftly, Thea's voice breaking.

'A folly . . . but one couldn't judge Vicky by everyday standards.' He didn't move to Thea's side, or make any attempt to persuade her.

'And what will the inquest reveal?' She added, 'You don't seem to be concerned about that—only the question of suicide.'

'One can fight revelations should there be any—the other, never.'

Thea's hands were clenched in her lap.

'I only know that I couldn't go on without you. I died inside when you said, earlier, that I was free.'

Julian hurried to her side, sat down beside her and put his arms around her shoulders, drawing her to him.

'I swear you'll never regret it. You'll have my love, loyalty and fidelity for ever, my darling.'

'And you shall have mine—no matter what happens at the inquest.' Whatever the price she might have to pay, she realised she would pay it rather than live without him.

'And no waiting until the end of the year,' he said with determination.

Thea met his gaze enquiringly. 'What have you in mind?'

'Special licence; a quiet wedding, almost immediately, perhaps at Amberley church—just Trevor and Robert as witnesses.'

Thea looked amazed and trembled slightly.

'Amberley church?' she echoed, and added quietly, 'That magnificent yew by the door . . . yes, I like that. Trevor will too.' She thought of Robert and rather dreaded telling him.

'I want desperately to make love to you,' Julian said hoarsely, 'but I also have a desire to make love to my *wife* . . . something romantic and——'

Faint colour rose in her cheeks and she curved back into his arms, aware of his sensitivity, while sharing his emotions.

'And now,' he said, 'I'd better go, or else I shan't be able to . . .' He got up swiftly and drew her to her feet.

'Bless you, my darling,' he said softly, kissing her. 'Good night.'

And with that he was gone.

*   *   *

Trevor did not betray his surprise when told of the wedding plans. A slight pain crossed his chest, as emotion struck. He had not been altogether satisfied with Julian's and Thea's attitude since their engagement, feeling it was strained. Now, suddenly, an altogether different atmosphere had crept into the proceedings, and he was more than thankful.

Robert heard the news with acute dismay, his expression hardening, his eyes almost accusing, as he said, 'You've been in love with him all along!'

Thea didn't prevaricate.

'Yes. From time to time I've tried to deceive myself, but—' she hesitated, 'I've never led you to believe that I loved you, I *do* love you—as a friend, Robert, and heaven knows, I've wished so often that I could be in love with you.'

There was an uneasy silence between them. He knew what she said was true, but he was worried nevertheless.

'I don't like it,' he said almost sternly. 'I don't like it at all.'

She stared at him, her heart racing as fear struck.

'What do you mean—*like* it?'

He sighed deeply. They were sitting in her office at the end of a heavy day. Miss Jenkins and Enid had gone, and Julian was at the hospital.

'The general situation. Look, Thea, Julian is my friend and partner, but I haven't pretended to understand him during this past year. Doesn't it strike you that he may be hastening the marriage to placate Lionel in case anything untoward comes out at the inquest? In the event of it being suicide, everything would be dragged into the glare of publicity—certainly the state of the Holford marriage.'

Thea gave a little angry cry.

'If that were true, he would have told me,' she insisted. 'You're not being fair because you're——' she
stumbled and didn't finish the sentence.

'Because I'm jealous?' He gave a little derisive grunt.
'Oh, I'm jealous all right—I'll admit that. I just don't
want to see you get hurt—marry a man who in reality
was in love with another woman and is now——'

'And you call yourself Julian's *friend*?'

'Not at this moment. I'm a man who loves you and
puts you before friendship.'

Thea sat there, cold, uncertain. There was logic in
what he had said, and then she thought of her words to
Julian such a short while before—a repetition of *his*
sentiments, love, loyalty and fidelity. If she was going to
falter now, what use her vow if it didn't include trust?

'Then you must let me live my own life as I think fit,'
Thea told him. 'I love Julian and I trust him. Whatever
the inquest discloses, and were Julian to be dragged into
it in any way, I should be prepared to stand by him and
be glad I was his wife.'

Robert wasn't satisfied.

'Julian owes it to you—and as a matter of fact, to me
too—to explain this whole situation. His silence is——'

'Something I accept.'

'You'll be living in Vicky's shadow, no matter what
you say.'

Thea shuddered, a sensation of fear touched her.
Wasn't Robert holding up a mirror reflecting a picture
from which she shrank?

She dropped her gaze and then asked jerkily, 'Would
you give *me* up rather than face the same shadow?'

He didn't hesitate. 'No.' The word came harshly, as he

added, 'I'd take the risk and allow for being a fool.'

She sighed deeply. 'Dear Robert.' It was a whisper. 'I'm so sorry to have caused you pain.'

He crossed to her desk as she sat at it, and kissed her forehead.

'I shall always be here,' he said quietly.

'And will you come to my wedding?'

'I'll do even that,' he promised.

There was a feeling of unreality during the following days. Plans had to be made, the practice affairs allowed for, Robert ready to fit in with any arrangements, while disapproving of the haste. It was when it came to fixing the actual date that Julian, much to Thea's surprise, hesitated. It seemed a contradiction after his initial eagerness, and she found herself tensing; woman-like, wildly jumping to the conclusion that he was regretting his precipitate action, when he said almost abruptly, 'I understand that the inquest is being held on the twenty-eighth. I'd like it to be over——' his voice trailed away, a shadow crossed his face. 'I was so anxious that we should be married quickly . . .'

'I'd thought of it,' she admitted, 'but——' She couldn't go into details without suspicion creeping in.

'I'd lost sight of time as such,' he admitted.

'Why not October—the second weekend?'

'You understand?' He looked anxious.

Thea could not tell him of her relief. It gave the lie to Robert's suggestion, which had not left her unmoved.

'Of course. One doesn't forget Vicky.' She met his gaze honestly and appreciated the fact that he didn't attempt to correct the statement. 'And I know that once Vicky's death had been proved an accident, you'll——' She stopped, finding that her emotions were to deeply involved to continue. The shadow of Vicky . . . would she ever lose it? Could she face up to it? Panic assailed her. If this was going to be her reaction at the first hurdle, what of the future? Robert's words re-echoed that, in effect, Julian owed her the truth. She cried inwardly because she knew that it was true and that while in a wild passionate moment it had not seemed to matter, now, facing a grim reality, it tore her apart.

'I've got the special licence,' he said. There was a note of near-triumph in his voice. 'The next thing is a real home. Ellsmere is fine for a bachelor, but we want our own roots?' He looked at her questioningly.

'Oh, yes,' she agreed thankfully, dreading lest he might have wanted to remain where he was.

He looked at his watch; they had had a light supper at her flat and he had a visit to make on his way home.

'This is what I hate,' he said, 'leaving you——'

They stood slightly apart, eyes meeting eyes; knowing that while he had to go, he could return . . .

He said, almost gruffly, 'I'm not going to spoil that moment.' He added, 'I won't make love to you and then leave you.' He drew her passionately to him, parted her lips in a long ecstatic kiss and then exclaimed with a wry smile as he reached the door of the sitting room, 'Saved by a patient!' Their gazes deepened and an ominous silence fell. Julian had also nearly been ruined by one, and the thought flashed dangerously between them.

A verdict of accidental death was returned at the inquest today on Mrs Lionel Holford, whose car, with her in it, went over the cleft at the Devil's Dyke on September 7th. Giving evidence, her husband said that she was accustomed to taking a picnic there and loved the spot. They were happily married and had planned, and made all preparations, to go to Venice on the Orient Express within a few days of the tragedy. The evidence was supported by Mr and Mrs Briggs, the Holfords' employees. Mrs Briggs had prepared sandwiches and a flask of coffee for Mrs Holford on the day of the accident, as she had done on many other occasions.

Postcards stamped and addressed to various friends, written by Mrs Holford, were found in the car, saying how much she was looking forward to going to Venice and that she would send the recipients a card *en route*. There were no circumstances to suggest other than accidental death caused as a result of her using the accelerator instead of the brake when about to turn and leave the picnic spot, after having released the handbrake.

The court expressed its sympathy to her husband.

Although Julian had heard the verdict over the local radio, it did not sink in until he actually saw the words in print in the early evening newspaper. His face was pale, but there was relief in the sadness that shadowed his expression, and Thea said, 'Now you can have peace of mind.'

He looked at her and there was a strange thankfulness in his voice as he said, 'Yes; that's a very good way to describe it.'

Thea felt he was suffering nevertheless, and she could

not share his grief which set him apart and isolated her from him in a way which hurt.

'You've got Mrs Burke to see,' she reminded him. 'I checked her over yesterday.'

'You sound serious.'

'I think she's having ovarian trouble. She's lost half a stone and isn't well. Blood pressure's raised and slight temperature. She isn't the type to go to bed unless sent there.' Thea knew Julian was grateful for the professional diversion. But words chased through her head: *In just a fortnight you'll be married to this man, and at this moment he seems a stranger locked in a world called "Vicky".*' Was she mad? Was——?

'Thea!' It was a sharp, anxious exclamation.

She felt as if cold water was being poured over her flesh.

'Yes?' It was a faint sound.

'You're not having second thoughts about—us?'

'No,' she said convincingly.

'Then tell Enid to bring Mrs Burke in.' Julian added as he reached the door, 'All I want now is for you to be Mrs Fraser.'

'You'll have to wait just over a fortnight for that,' she warned him, and for the first time they smiled.

It was one of those early October days, a Saturday, when Julian and Thea were married, and Keats' words, *'Season of mists and mellow fruitfulness'*, expressed the enchantment of autumn, when the world was sprinkled with gold dust. Amberley church, with its magnificent yew which had been moved over two hundred years ago from the vicarage garden, when it was then about three hundred years old, set the scene much as it was in the thirteenth century, the tower rising nobly behind the castle wall.

As Thea stood at the altar, her love for Julian welled up to deaden her nerves and leave her with only the happiness of being there with him. And when the service was over and they walked down the aisle together, all the relief, hope and ecstasy mingled to give her smile a radiance as she turned and met his adoring gaze. Trevor swallowed hard, and Robert looked straight ahead. He thought how vulnerable Thea looked in her cream suit with its tucked silk blouse, and bouquet of matching roses.

They returned to Hove to Julian's flat, where they were to spend the first night before flying to Madeira the following day.

Trevor managed to have a few seconds alone with Thea.

'I have something for you,' he said with a quiet gravity as he handed her an envelope. 'Vicky gave it to me to give you on your wedding day—if you married Julian.'

'Vicky?' Thea's heart seemed to miss a beat and a pang shot through her. The sun seemed suddenly to have gone in, and the dark clouds of thunder take its place. Why should Vicky write to her? 'When?'

'The week of the accident,' he said. 'She came and gave it to me personally. In the event of your not marrying Julian, I was to tear it up . . . Julian was not to know anything about it . . . sh-h!' Trevor walked away as he heard Julian's voice. Thea managed to hurry into the bedroom and slip the letter into her handbag.

It was not until Julian was showering after Trevor and Robert had gone that Thea had a few minutes alone to read it. Vicky had written,

'Thea, very dear,

Unless I write this you'll never know the truth.
Julian isn't the type of man ever to let me down by
excusing himself at my expense, and if you don't
love him enough to take him on trust, then you're
not worthy of him and you will never read this
letter.

I pursued him, lovingly rather than aggressive-
ly, and he cared enough for me to be sorry for me,
with a sadness not pity. I almost ruined him, with
my increasing medical demands, following him
wherever he went, or where I thought I might be
lucky enough to meet him. I had an ulterior
motive in this respect even where my friendship
with you and Robert was concerned.

My life was empty and he filled it. I didn't
belong anywhere, and my money meant nothing.
As for my marriage——'

Thea paused as she read, her heart thudding; she could
hear Vicky speaking, *see* her——

'I didn't love Lionel and as time went by I didn't
even *like* him. I think I once said to you that he
bought me everything, but gave me nothing.
After that time in hospital, when I'd inevitably
seen more of Julian than normal, I found I
couldn't live without him. I was in a highly nervous state, which he recognised, and my attitude
endangered his position as a doctor. He said that
unless I behaved like a patient and a normal
friend, he would refuse to look after me. I threatened suicide and often feigned being ill, or
unwell, just in order to see him.

Then Lionel became suspicious, but even that didn't seem to matter. I felt quite reckless. That time in the hospital when I called him *darling*—I *knew* what I was saying; and just before I was ill, I deliberately clasped his hand in the swimming pool. Little things, but capable of destroying him. I even tried to kiss him, and you noticed the lipstick. And all the time, Lionel's suspicions were increasing.

The crisis came when I went to Julian's flat that night, to make a last desperate effort to persuade him to come away with me. He'd shown me kindness, and I built up every little gesture and normal act, until I'd convinced myself that he loved me in return. I begged him to take me away, as I've said. I was completely unstable and he told me that this was the end; that he would cease to be my doctor from that moment on; that he couldn't endure the strain any longer. He begged me to begin a new life with Lionel, have a child. I told him I only wanted *his* child. And then you came in. Lionel was intent upon ruining Julian and would have done so but for your announcement of your engagement. Lionel was very suspicious of that.

But . . . when you read this, dear Thea, I shall be dead—I can't go on without Julian in my life, without seeing him, hearing his voice. I can't live in Lionel's "money" world, but even knowing what lies ahead makes me calm and at peace. If I've done nothing else except love Julian, then I shall not have lived in vain.

I've planned it all; willed myself to be a good wife

during these months. Arranged the trips to the
Devil's Dyke which, as you know, I do love. No
loose ends. The verdict must never be suicide,
because that would place an intolerable burden
on Julian and put him at Lionel's mercy.

I wanted Julian's happiness so deeply, and that
happiness lies with you. He didn't realise he was
in love with you, but will do so, and my only fear
is lest you should not love him enough. He's a
very fine man; an honourable man, Thea . . .
love him as I would give my life to do. My *life* . . .
In the end it was all I had *to* give to set him free.

Thank you for being you, and for
your friendship,
Vicky.'

Thea dashed the tears from her eyes and knew she
must postpone her grieving. The precious moments that
lay ahead must be given wholly to Julian. Swiftly she slid
out of her clothes and put on the brocade housecoat she
had worn the night Julian told her he loved her. Just
then he came out of the bathroom, wearing a sapphire
silk dressing gown, and looked approvingly at her
appearance.

Champagne was in the ice-bucket, and he poured out
two glasses, as though drawing out the moments in order
to savour them. The evening and night were theirs.

'To my wife,' he said as he raised his glass. His gaze
held hers with a passionate earnestness.

'To my husband,' whispered Thea, almost shyly.

They sipped and put down their glasses as she moved
into his arms, his kiss long and rapturous—filled with a
desire only surrender could fulfil.

Then, drawing back, he said intently, 'Thea, my darling, trust me; never let the past be a shadow, *please*.'

She clung to him and her voice throbbed with sincerity as she thought of Vicky.

'I trust you with my life, and there will never be any shadows,' she promised.

He kissed the top of her head.

'Don't you think you're rather overdressed?' he said whimsically.

She stood back slightly and let her housecoat slip from her shoulders, to reveal her perfect body.

'That's soon remedied,' she smiled as they moved towards the bed . . .

SPOT THE COUPLE

AND WIN A

£1,000

REAL PEARL NECKLACE

PLUS 10 PAIRS OF REAL PEARL EAR STUDS WORTH OVER £100 EACH

A

B

No piece of jewellery is more romantic than the soft glow and lustre of a real pearl necklace, pearls that grow mysteriously from a grain of sand to a jewel that has a romantic history that can be traced back to Cleopatra and beyond.

To enter just study Photograph A showing a young couple. Then look carefully at Photograph B showing the same section of the river. Decide where you think the couple are standing and mark their position with a cross in pen.

Complete the entry form below and mail your entry PLUS TWO OTHER "SPOT THE COUPLE" Competition Pages from June, July or August Mills and Boon paperbacks, to Spot the Couple, Mills and Boon Limited, Eton House, 18/24 Paradise Road, Richmond, Surrey, TW9 1SR, England. All entries must be received by December 31st 1988.

ENTRY FORM

Name _____

Address _____

_____

I bought this book in TOWN _____ COUNTRY _____

This offer applies only to books purchased outside the UK & Eire.
You may be mailed with other offers as a result of this application.